T. Csernis & Julia Bland

THE HUNT FOR NIEDREID
A NUMEN CHRONICLES INTERLUDE STORY

ORIGINAL EDITION

GLOSSARY

Ethos [ee-thos] - The energy within someone that can be used to create or manipulate other energies

✝

Dor-Sanguis [door-san-goo-wis] - Translates roughly to Pain *[Portuguese]* and blood *[Latin]*
(aka, Romania)

✝

Nefastus [neh-fas-tus] – Translates to Unlawful *[Latin]*
(aka, the Americas)

✝

Eltaria [el-tar-ia] – Zalith's homeworld

✝

Numen [noo-men] - God-like beings that chose to show themselves to the world rather than remain anonymous

✝

Aegis [ee-gis] - The Dragon Gods, children of Letholdus

✝

DeiganLupus [day-gan-loo-pus] - Translates roughly to 'refused to turn to the wolf' *[Icelantic, Latin]*
(aka, UK)

✝

Lumendatt [loo-men-dat] – Numen crystals containing the power to create life

✝

Obcasus [ob-cass-us] – Knives capable of putting Numen in a frozen statis

✝

Proselytus [pros-elly-tus] – A heart-like organ which creates ethos inside a body

✝

Scion [skee-on] – ethos-crafted children of the Numen

✝

Infățișare [in-fuh-tsee-SHAH-reh] – vampires able to shift into animal forms

✝

The Seven Realms:

Aegisguard [ee-gis-guard] - The world
(aka, Earth)
Mareaeternum [Mar-ay-ter-num] Translates to eternal tide *[Latin]*
Glaciaqua [Glass-ee-aqua]
Letholdus [Lee-fold-us]
Tengetso [Ten-get-so]
Celitrianas [Sel-it-ree-a-nas]
Yilmana [Yeel-mana]

The Months and Currency

Months

January – Primis
February – Cordus
March – Tertium
April – Aprilis
May – Quintus
June – Iunius
July – Quintilis
August – Tria
September – Novem
October – Decem
November – Undecim
December – Clausula

Currency

Copper – Equivalent of $0.01
Bronze – Equivalent of $0.20
Silver – Equivalent of $2
Gold – Equivalent of $10
Coronam – Equivalent of $100
Cidaris – Equivalent of $1 million

CONTENTS

Understanding Alucard's Accent

Alucard's dialogue in this edition of the story has an accent. He doesn't pronounce Hs, THs and some Rs. Below are some examples to help you understand his dialogue:

You'll see words like 'ead (head), 'ere (here), and 'owever (however), missing the H.

THs are often ZHs, such as zhat (that), zhis (this), zhe (the), and zhere (there). In other cases, you'll see ozzer (other).

Ws become Vs, such as vhat (what), vhere (where), and vhy (why).

Some Ds become Zs, such as Zamien (Damien), zon't (don't), and Zetlaff (Detlaff).

Fs also become Vs, such as vollow (follow), vriend (friend), and vor (for).

And some Rs become Vs, such as vest (rest), Veiner (Reiner), and Remont (Vemont).

Understanding POV Date and Location

How you'll see a new POV change laid out:

| Alucard—*Tuesday, Tertium 28th, 960(TG)* |
| *Vharakaal, Eshkunda, Anaket, Thaleus Village* |

What the hell does this layout mean?

| Name of whose POV it is—*Day, Month, Year(Period)* |
| *Continent, Country, Province, The Place in the Province* |

↓ And what about this? ↓

⇄ Zalith

These are quick POV flips during fast-paced scenes such as battles, letting you catch what the other characters are going through without breaking the flow

Chapter One

— ⊰ ✝ ⊱ —

Made to Choose

| *Alucard—Sunday, Decem 23rd, 537(TG)—423 Years Ago* |
| *Rhenovaalis, Dor-Sanguis, Sanguine Castle, The Lucidian Catacombs* |

Until today, Aleksei hadn't really thought too much about how they were different from the other kids. The fangs, the scales, the claws—sure, those things were obvious and always had been. But now? As they stood amidst the crowd of children in the centre of the inspection hall waiting for the priestesses to begin grouping them up, the confusion about who they were grew heavier.

That confusion, however, clashed with the unease constricting their heart.

The inspection hall was probably the most intimidating of places in this lightless, endless maze of tunnels, and not just because of the crimson stains and the chill that lingered there, colder than anywhere else. Above, the ceiling arched high, vanishing into darkness that no torch or spell ever seemed to reach. Cold stone pillars loomed along the walls, carved with spiralling runes that pulsed faintly, and the bloodstained floor was made of uneven slabs, darker in some places, as if the stone had grown used to pain and now revelled in it.

Children had died in this place. Aleksei once heard whispers among the others that some would rather die here than melt away or crumble when they attempted the ritual— Aleksei would be lying if they said they hadn't thought the same thing once or twice…perhaps more…but those were just fleeting thoughts. They couldn't die. They had to live, they had to serve Lilith.

The priestesses huddled by the door, whispering, smirking, laughing. Some of them were pregnant—at least half of them always were, and Aleksei understood the reason now. When Abbess Brânduśa stepped into the room, though, the women fell into an obedient silence.

Brânduśa looked around at them all before adorning a skeptical frown. "Where's Voichiţa?" she questioned.

The priestesses shot each other unsure frowns.

"And Despina?" the Abbess asked, sounding angrier.

Once again, the women looked confused.

Aleksei's heart raced even harder now. Despina and Voichiţa's absence had already been noticed. While their bodies wouldn't be found, Aleksei was worried that their disappearances might make things harder for them. Then again…they'd learned to hide in the gloom. But that didn't take away the anxiety.

They watched as Brânduśa stormed off, her robes trailing behind her like a torn shadow. The other priestesses followed at a slower pace, whispering among themselves. Moments later, the familiar routine began; serrated commands rang out as the children were gathered and sorted.

The first two groupings always eluded Aleksei; for years, the logic behind them was a mystery. But after reading that book, the truth had begun to take shape: the children were first organized by the priestess who had created them, and then—more quietly—by the male who contributed. Those were the candidates for the beginning of new sire lines, weren't they?

Aleksei was never called into either group. They remained alone, set apart. Their mother was dead, and if she had created others, they were long gone, erased or discarded. No siblings, no lineage, no place. Just the corner. Just them.

Half in shadow, half forgotten, they observed as the children were next herded into lines by the barking priestesses. Age order, as always. Those who hesitated or didn't know their birthdates were met with swift correction: a thin wooden rod that struck with a sharp crack across knuckles or wrists. Some were cut, not just struck—the tip of the stick splintered at the end, sharp enough to bite. Crimson dotted the floor in seconds, joining faded stains that had never quite washed away. The air filled with the deep tang of fresh blood and muffled sobs as the youngest trembled in place, trying not to draw attention.

Aleksei knew their birthday. They made sure to remember because it was the last time they heard their mother's voice, and the first and last time they saw her face. But as the years went by, those memories slowly weakened. They grasped onto whatever they had left, though. No matter what happened, they'd not forget her.

It was the final sorting that always left Aleksei drifting and uncertain. The priestesses called for the boys to stand on the left and the girls to the right, splitting everything into two neat halves.

But where would they stand?

They glanced between the groups, heart knocking quietly in their chest. They weren't one or the other—not really. Nothing about them felt entirely like either side. Were they both? Neither? Something else entirely? The thought twisted in their stomach, not from fear exactly but from the weight of not knowing.

Was this what Gossamer meant when they said that Aleksei was different?

With a confounded frown, they thought harder. Was there a moment coming when they'd be forced to choose? Or worse, when someone else would choose for them?

The idea made them feel stranger than they already did. Would they have to choose?

Their attention was stolen by painful winces and the thickening scent of blood.

The priestesses started the inspection.

First came the blood, thin sticks drawn across skin to test obedience, to see who flinched, who cried. The ones who couldn't name their birthdates bled the most, more and more every time they still couldn't answer. The priestesses just laughed and yelled, and Brânduśa stood there with a satisfied smirk on her ugly, wart-covered face.

All the blood might capture Aleksei's senses if they weren't so afraid.

Then it was time for recitations. Doctrine and oaths. Aleksei mouthed along but never spoke aloud. Speaking meant being seen—not that anything would come of it. They always ensured that they were prepared, but they were never asked to recite; this was one of many things that made them think the Abbess and priestesses wanted them to fail. That didn't stop them from learning what they could from observing, though. Lilith wouldn't be at all impressed to hear that they'd failed inspection.

Next, the pain threshold trials began. A glance, a nod, and a priestess would press a curse-marked brand to a child's arm. The ones who screamed were marked for reconditioning, and those who tried to be strong but cried were struck with that same bloodied stick. Every child's hands were covered in cuts at this point.

Then ethos. Older children summoned shadow or etched sigils in the air, their wounded hands shaking. One child—Tudosia, Aleksei was sure her name was—never passed this test. Every time she tried creating a sigil, the ethos backfired, sending sparks across the hall, and her hands were always torn open after the test. This time, though, the wounds were more severe, and Tudosia passed out.

Seeing her dragged to a corner and tossed away like some unwanted thing made Aleksei feel sick—it made them feel the urge to go to her…almost as if it were instinct. But they knew that if they moved, they'd end up just like her.

The final test came around—the readiness check. The worst part. No blood, no bruises, just quiet murmurs and long looks from the inspectors, their rings glowing as they passed them over exposed skin, ensuring that each child was still what Aleksei had heard the priestesses call 'pure'. They didn't know what that meant, though…only that those who didn't fit whatever checklist the priestesses had…they—

"Tainted filth!" a priestess yelled, yanking an older boy forward.

Again, Aleksei felt the urge to help, but they couldn't. All they could do was watch as the boy pleaded for his life, dragged to the other end of the hall, and with a single stab of the same knife that killed the others, the boy went silent.

Aleksei looked away, trying to take their mind off it. Despite having witnessed the deaths of so many of the others, they never got used to it—they didn't want to.

Footsteps clicked across the stone. Aleksei didn't have to look to know who they belonged to.

Abbess Brânduśa.

Her presence curdled the air before she even spoke. The hem of her robe swept too close to Aleksei's feet as she came to a stop, and her shadow fell across them like a shroud. "You manage to look more disgusting every time I have to see you," she said, her voice syrupy with disdain. "Why we still keep you around is beyond me. But Lady Lilith continues to insist that we don't let you wither and die," the woman grumbled.

Aleksei kept their eyes forward. If they looked up, she'd smile—she always smiled when they reacted, giving her an excuse to strike them. But it wasn't only the avoidance of pain that kept them from making a sound. Lilith wanted them kept alive. The thought pushed aside some of the angst. But with that hopeful feeling came the same confusion that Aleksei had felt when in the library not too long ago. Why was Lilith here? Why did their mother serve her within a cult that worshipped Lucifer?

Without warning, Brânduśa's first strike came harshly across Aleksei's knuckles with her ringed hand.

Snapping out of their thoughts, Aleksei bit down on the whimper rising in their throat, fingers curling tight.

Brânduśa clicked her tongue. "You still haven't learned to answer when addressed. How disappointing." She reached into her sleeve and pulled out a thin, jagged stick— rune-carved, splintered at the tip.

Aleksei's stomach twisted.

"Hand," she said.

They gave it to her. They always did.

When the stick sliced a shallow line across Aleksei's palm, they noticed that the runes on it weren't the same as those used on the other children. They'd never really looked before, but now they had a reason to take in more than just the obvious details.

Why, though?

Blood welled up from the cut bright and fast, and although Aleksei's jaw trembled, they didn't cry. They'd avoid giving Brânduśa what she wanted for as long as they possibly could.

The Abbess studied the cut, and then she turned their hand palm-up towards the torchlight, murmuring something under her breath. The blood shimmered unnaturally, reacting to the runes. She looked pleased. "You remain useful," she said flatly. "For now."

Then came the pain threshold test. She pressed two fingers to their wrist, whispering a curse too low to catch—but the ethos understood. Pain surged up Aleksei's arm like ice driven through bone, twisting as it climbed to their shoulder. It felt as though something had burrowed beneath their skin, dragging heat and cold behind it in equal measure.

Aleksei hissed, the sound slipping out before they could swallow it.

Brânduśa leaned in, breath warm and cloying against their cheek. "There it is," she whispered cruelly. "Always so brave and conceited…until it hurts. Just like your mother."

Their hands clenched into fists, claws digging into their palms as the pain began to ebb, leaving a bitter ache in its wake. Shame flared hotter than the ethos and deeper than the sting. But they didn't act upon the rising instinct to fight back and defend themself. They didn't fall or cry or beg for her to stop. They stayed standing—barely; they fought against their body, resisting the enticement to give in. It would be so easy to give up and collapse, but they had to prove themself—not to these people, but to Lilith.

No recitations and oaths.

No aptitude showcase.

The readiness check, though. Brânduśa took great pleasure in that. She examined Aleksei closely, the rings around her fingers glowing brightly as disgust contorted her face. Every time she did this, Aleksei's heart raced hard in their chest, dreading that this might be the time the Abbess declared them impure.

But despite her usual anxious, horrified response, Brânduśa always did the same thing—a harsh, revolted scoff as she let go of Aleksei's arm with a flick and huff. A demeaning glare, and something else lingered in her crimson eyes, but Aleksei didn't know what to call that expression…or emotion.

Every inspection ended the same way, too.

Priestesses Irinaşca, Radmila, and Mărioara emerged from the large wooden door that sat between two tall pillars alight with orange flames. With them, they carried that…thing. The Eye. A waist-high winged statue carved from golden stone and veined red with something that pulsed faintly beneath the surface. Its face was fierce and starved, and its eyes stared endlessly, rimmed with silver and set with glowing crimson gems.

It didn't blink.

It didn't move.

But it saw.

This time, Aleksei joined the crowd, dragged by their wrist, not fighting, not resisting…as much as they wanted to.

Once the priestesses lifted the statue and placed it on the altar, the children were made to step forward one by one, to stand before The Eye in silence.

The statue didn't need questions. It simply looked—and it knew.

Aleksei stood at the end of the line, hands cold, chest tight. The memory of the last boy who failed The Eye still hovered like a ghost in the hall—he'd trembled too hard, looked away, and when The Eye flared red, the priestesses didn't even hesitate. They'd hauled him off screaming, and he was executed…just like the others.

And the same thing happened again now.

Three children. Aleksei only knew one of their names.

A girl no older than six—Dragana…or maybe it was Dargana.

Not knowing for sure made Aleksei feel guilty…even if they weren't supposed to. There was a rule—Lilith's rule—one she never failed to remind them of whenever their paths crossed, which was rarer than Aleksei would have liked.

'Don't care about the others. Don't look at them like they matter. They're not your equals. They're not your kin.'

Every child here was either going to die or disappear. That was the truth, one that Aleksei knew now more than ever, so what was the point in pretending any of them meant something?

Aleksei had tried to obey. Once. Sometimes, they still tried. But lately, Lilith's voice wasn't the only one in their head. Another had joined it—quieter, gentler, more like a whisper in the dark, yet loud enough to make them hesitate.

They liked to think that it was their mother's voice, as if she was somehow still with them after death. Was that even possible?

Pleading, crying voices snapped them out of their thoughts.

The second kid The Eye flared at was a boy with a split lip—his name was a mystery…one never heard nor spoken.

And the third was another whose hands kept shaking—again…unnameable.

All three stepped up, and all three failed.

The Eye pulsed red with each one, and the priestesses prowled towards them like starved beasts, fangs bared and ready to tear.

There was no trial, no hesitation. The executions were swift. Ritualized. Their blood hit the stone like a signature, each slain with that same knife, each disposed of in that same part of the hall.

Aleksei's turn crept closer. They didn't flinch or let their thoughts scatter; they kept their mind quiet. Not empty—empty minds raised suspicion, too. Just quiet enough. And when they stood before The Eye, it felt like the thing crawled into their chest, turning over every secret, every half-formed rebellion, every whispered fear.

They could feel those things meant to be buried trying to creep in, like The Eye was turning over stones, hunting. But Aleksei wouldn't think about earlier—they locked onto the thought of Lilith, of making her proud, of making her see their true potential. That thought was ever-present, strong enough to bury everything else.

The Eye didn't flare. It let Aleksei go, and its watchful, glowing gaze began examining a girl it had just assessed…all because she coughed lightly, probably because of the bruises on her neck.

Aleksei stepped back, letting their heart pound before attempting to calm down. For now, The Eye had passed them over. But the feeling of it lingered, like ash ensnaring the inside of their skull.

Moments later, The Eye let the girl go, and the statue went silent.

Four children had died this time, two less than the inspection before.

How long ago was that?

Aleksei couldn't recall. Time blurred together in this place. The only concept they had of it was when they needed blood and the wait in between feeds.

"Get them back to their cages," Brânduśa said to the priestesses as she headed for the door. "And find Despina and Voichiţa." And then she left, taking with her most of the heavy, oppressive tension.

"Move it," the priestesses began barking.

Aleksei slipped into the crowd of sniffling, silent children. No one spoke. They only exchanged fleeting glances. A few of the older ones offered the younger children soft looks, a hand on a shoulder when the priestesses weren't looking, and the barest nod of reassurance. They didn't really know each other. No friendships, no bonds. None of them ever looked at Aleksei with anything but confusion or quiet irritation. Still…what was the word? Admiration. Yes. Aleksei admired the way they all tried—however clumsily—to come together, to pretend that things might be okay.

Even when they all knew the truth.

It wasn't.

Chapter Two

— ⸲ † ⸳ —

When, If At All?

| **Alucard**—*Friday, Aprilis 14th, 960(TG)* |
| *Aestrael, Uzlia Isles, Usrul, Castle Reiner* |

That was when Alucard stirred.

He tossed and turned in bed, but the thumping in his head made it hard for him to get comfortable. And the dream? That didn't help, either. Abbess Brânduśa was long-dead—he knew that—but seeing her face…dream or not…it made him feel sick. It made his chest feel tight.

Or maybe it was what he'd been thinking in that moment. While he watched all the other children be sorted and categorized, he'd just stood there, not knowing where he belonged, asking himself if he'd have to choose one or the other eventually.

When had he chosen? He still hadn't remembered that moment. All he kept recalling were memories like this. Memories of his time in those catacombs, memories of Gossamer, but no memories that explained to him why he felt the way he did right now. No memories that helped him feel comfortable in his own skin. No memories that helped him escape the heavy, suffocating feeling that he wasn't a real man, that he was just some…*thing*—that he was inferior, and that he'd never be able to give Zalith the things he deserved, the things that Zalith gave *him*.

He scowled and rolled onto his right side, trying to banish the weight of his thoughts, but they clung stubbornly. His gaze landed on Zalith's face, softened in sleep, and his heart twisted with an ache he couldn't shake. He should have been drowning in the intense pull and the demanding instincts, feeling only the urge pulling him closer. Instead, his mind betrayed him.

Zalith looked every bit man—strong, defined, effortlessly certain even in repose. The sharp line of his jaw, the sculpted planes of his face, the way even sleep did nothing to dull the commanding presence he carried. He was what Alucard imagined a man was meant to be.

And then there was himself.

Alucard's fingers drifted, almost without thought, to his own jaw—*again*. It was too soft and slight, caught between something masculine and something else he could never quite claim; not the elegance Zalith wore so naturally but a strangeness that he couldn't unsee…a reminder that he wasn't whole. Not the way Zalith was.

He stared until his chest tightened, bordering on suffocating, until the contrast burned. Zalith was everything he wasn't: real, definite, and undeniably male.

And Alucard…wasn't.

Despite that staring only made him feel worse with each passing moment, he couldn't look away. His eyes stayed fixed, dragging comparison after comparison he wished he could silence. It had become a pattern, a cruel ritual he couldn't stop, and since Atheson, it had become relentless.

He couldn't shake the fear that Zalith's reassurances had only been pity, soft words to keep from breaking him. The thought gnawed at him in every quiet moment, especially when they were together. Especially when they had sex. That was when the inferiority cut deepest, when Zalith's strength and certainty only highlighted everything Alucard wasn't. It had sunk so far into him that even the pull of heat had dulled beneath it. What should have been fire felt more like smoke, thin and fading. The urges still lingered, tethering him close to desire, but it was more edge than flame, a reminder of what he should want rather than what he truly did.

With a despondent sigh, he closed his eyes and tried to let sleep claim him again.

But all he could see was Brânduśa's face. All he could hear was her voice.

And all he could feel was the despair of not knowing who or what he was.

He opened his eyes, staring at Zalith once again.

Even when his mate sluggishly turned onto his back, he stared at the side of his face. There *was* desire beneath everything else—beneath the admiration and the dismay and…yes, he was jealous. How could he not be? He wished he looked as masculine as the man beside him. But he didn't want to focus on all of that. He considered letting his urges win and waking Zalith for sex; he knew that his mate would be *very* happy to oblige; however, Alucard knew that it would only make him feel worse. The pleasure would only distract him for so long, probably not as long as usual thanks to the memory that had been resurfacing.

So he rolled onto his back and sighed—his scars twinged in response, sending burning pain through his body, forcing him to roll onto his other side with an irritated huff…and then onto his front, easing his arms under his pillow. He felt both restless and drained, trapped in a state that felt like its own private hell. It was like an itch buried too deep to scratch, something crawling beneath his skin that refused to be shaken loose. The only way to free himself of the parasite was to drink poison, silver laced with hemlock and poppy resin and surripio.

No. That was an extreme overexaggeration—cruel, even. The missing pieces and disconnection with himself weren't *that* terrible, and neither was the despair that came with it all, nor the cure to the desperation. It was the fact that it bled into the moments that were supposed to matter most. He wanted Zalith. Fuck, he wanted him *so fucking badly*. He craved the closeness and reassurance and the safety of being wrapped in his arms. Sex had always been a tether to Alucard, the language that bound them when words fell short. But every time, because of this unrelenting feeling of inferiority, the sweetness soured; every kiss carried the aftertaste of inadequacy, and every touch seemed to underline how strange and wrong he felt in his own skin. He loved the intimacy, he *needed* it, but being unable to lose himself in it without dysphoria clawing at him made him want to tear himself apart.

That was the word he'd been searching for. Dysphoria. The name for the shadow gnawing at him.

He let out a slow breath and turned his gaze to the darkened room. Kaleidoscopic moonlight fractured through the cracks in the curtains, scattering in pale ribbons across the walls, while the soft patter of rain against the balcony doors wove itself into the stillness. The sound should have been calming—in some way, it was; the tension in his shoulders loosened, his body softened into the sheets, and sleep began to circle him like a predator closing in—but the desire didn't fade. It lingered, twisting inside him like smoke in his lungs.

His body demanded that he give it what it craved, louder and louder with every heartbeat… and that was the cruellest part: wanting, yet not wanting. His instincts begged for sex, for the relief of Zalith's touch, but his mind warped every image, turning everything unbearable. It was like trying to step into a skin that didn't fit, as if intimacy pulled taut the seams of a costume he wasn't meant to wear. Each touch risked tearing the disguise, exposing the strange, mismatched figure he could never quite escape.

The desire burned, the fear suffocated, and he lay trapped between them, caged in a body that felt both prison and imposter.

He sighed, restless, rolling onto his back only to twist aside again, as though motion alone could shake free the thoughts gnawing at him. But then came a darker idea: maybe if he stayed on his back, the discomfort would drown out the storm inside his head.

So he forced himself still, letting the full weight of his body press down. His scars burned immediately; the fabric scraped against ridges of half-healed flesh, dragging heat and sting where skin had never mended clean. The pain flared sharply and gradually settled into a slow, searing throb. This time, he didn't move. He let the ache spread, welcoming the irritation as it climbed like fire up his spine. He left his scars to suffer, clinging to the punishment as if it might smother the war raging louder inside.

But all that did was bring even more flashes of memory, reminding him of every time Damien and Lilith had whipped him, every time they'd beaten him.

He didn't want to think about that, either.

Once again, he rolled onto his side. Sleep wouldn't free him at all, not from the dysphoria, not from the pain and despair of memories. Whatever he did, he was going to have to deal with it in some shape or form.

Alucard carefully sat up, trying his best not to wake Zalith. Lying around in silence only amplified the struggle, so he got up, pulled on his trousers, and went over to the desk. As he sat down, he reached through a small rift and into his office; he took his memory journal, and then he opened it to the latest page. As much as these memories were upsetting him, he needed to write them down.

So he got to work, focusing on the rain and the scratching of his pen instead of the images that crept into his mind with each word he wrote. A part of him hoped that putting it all on paper would help him remember the moment he wanted to, but it didn't come. He didn't know when or if he'd chosen to be male—or as close as he was to it.

He felt the urge to find something that would let him see his reflection.

There was nothing, though. That was a good thing. He didn't need to be staring at himself and drawing attention to all the flaws.

He kept writing despite the number of times his hand stalled above the page, especially when it came to the more uncomfortable details, the ones that left his chest hollow and his stomach twisted. But he forced himself forward. He had to. If he couldn't look these truths in the eye, then what was the point? This was his past. No matter how much it burned, he couldn't escape it or bury it forever.

As he worked, though, the pain in his head came back. It started as a dull ache behind his eyes, and then it sharpened the longer he pressed the pen across the page. Each word dragged at him, splitting his focus between the sting in his temples and the gnawing weight inside him. Still, he wrote on, even as his vision blurred and the letters started to swim.

His hand slipped once, leaving an ugly blot of ink that bled into the paper. That was when his strength gave out. He dropped the pen, pressing his palm against his brow, trying to smother the pounding there. He felt wrung out, his body sluggish, his thoughts fraying into white noise.

This was enough for tonight.

He pushed the journal aside and stood up, swaying a little before taking his trousers off and making his way back to bed. The sheets felt cold when he slipped beneath them, but he was too tired to care. He curled onto his side, pressing his back against Zalith's warm body; the ache in his head dulled only slightly, and he let his eyes sink shut.

Sleep claimed him quickly, swallowing the words he'd forced himself to relive.

Would his dreams force him to relive it all again?

Probably. But there was nothing he could do to stop it.

Chapter Three

— ⸱ ✝ ⸱ —

Not Enough

| **Alucard—***Saturday, Aprilis 15th, 960(TG)* |
| *Uzlia Isles, Usrul, Castle Reiner* |

It was intense, blisteringly so; the kind of heat that clawed through muscle and marrow, the kind that blurred thought and stripped restraint until there was nothing left but desire. Alucard was lost in it, in *him*, in the way Zalith fidgeted beneath him with his face against his pillow, his body pinned down and slick with pheromones.

Every thrust dragged a low, pleased sound from the demon's throat, and Alucard moaned with him, spiralling deeper into the bliss. The scent of their sex clung to the air, thick and heady and laced with their natural aromas, those uniquely demonic fragrances that tangled together, intoxicating and maddening; Zalith's pheromones were rich and sweet, subtly corruptive, but they didn't stand a chance against Alucard's own—his heat had made sure of that.

The vampire leaned in, fangs grazing Zalith's neck as he ground deeper into him, burying his dick with every plunge, dragging a strangled gasp from his mate's lips. His fingers clamped around Zalith's wrists, hard enough to bruise, anchoring him as he rutted in again, further and rougher until the rhythm stopped being something he controlled and became something he obeyed.

Alucard's breath grew ragged, his limbs trembling from how close he was to coming undone. Zalith's body was divine under his, so hot, so tight, so perfect that he could weep from it.

And still, it wasn't enough.

A strained whine left the vampire as he kept thrusting, trying to hold on a little longer until he could push Zalith over the edge from nothing but his dick alone. He angled his hips and drove in aggressively, instincts clawing at him as he chased that elusive spot, desperate to feel the demon tremble and unravel. That was all he wanted, to make him cum like this, to stay in control long enough to hear his mate gasp his name the way he loved, to draw that pleasure from him with nothing but his body and his rhythm.

But the ache inside him was too much, the need too consuming.

His movements faltered. A cry tore from him as his climax surged up without mercy, snapping through his spine and leaving him breathless. He buried himself as deep as he could go and came *hard*, his whole body trembling as heat burst through him in searing pulses. For a moment, there was nothing but Zalith's warmth around him, his scent, the trembling of their bodies locked together.

Then came the silence.

Alucard collapsed forward, his chest rising and falling against Zalith's slick back. A dazed breath left him, but it didn't carry satisfaction. It carried defeat.

He blinked hard, trying to shake the haze, but the shame was already blooming beneath the surface. He hadn't meant to; he was supposed to hold out, to give Zalith everything. But once again, his body had betrayed him—just like always. The heat, the pheromones, the way he always lost control the moment he felt good—it was humiliating.

His throat tightened.

Why was it always so easy for Zalith to ruin him? Why couldn't he ever return the favour, at least not like this?

A bitter voice curled through his mind, louder now than it had been since they left Atheson, louder than last night. He was supposed to be a man—he was supposed to be Zalith's equal. But he couldn't even last long enough to make him cum. It hit harder than it should have…because somewhere deep down, it didn't feel like just a failure of control. It felt like proof that he wasn't enough, not man enough, not *anything* enough.

He didn't move. He just stayed there, his hands resting loosely over Zalith's wrists, eyes shut tight, pretending for a moment that he hadn't just disappointed them both.

Beneath him, Zalith let out a breathless, amused laugh. "Are you okay?"

Mortification twisted in Alucard's gut. He didn't want to talk—he didn't want to acknowledge it, least of all out loud. So he exhaled sharply through his nose and muttered, "Just catching my breath."

The demon gave another laugh, and then he shifted, drawing back just enough to slip free of Alucard's lax grip. Before the vampire could fully retreat, strong arms looped around him. In one swift motion, Zalith rolled them over, flipping Alucard onto his back and straddling him. His weight pinned the vampire down, holding him there easily.

"You're about to lose it again," Zalith said, smirking down at him—teasing, yes, but with a warmth that stung more than any cruelty.

Zalith leaned down and kissed him.

There was no hesitation, no gentleness, only heat and that familiar, grounding dominance that always managed to quiet the storm in Alucard's head. Their mouths met in a messy, desperate clash of lips and breath, tongues sliding, teeth grazing; for a few seconds, it was just that, the noise of their breathing, the press of their chests, and the wet, open-mouthed sound of their kiss deepening until Alucard couldn't tell if the ache in his gut was from embarrassment or arousal.

The demon broke the kiss with a low sound in his throat. He didn't speak as he reached down, one hand grasping Alucard's thigh to hook it high over his waist, dragging him closer. The other hand went between them, slick fingers moving eagerly. He didn't waste time teasing; he made sure Alucard was properly prepared—quick, lube-covered strokes, confident pressure—and then he was guiding his dick to Alucard's ass.

And with a steady thrust, Zalith slid in.

Alucard tensed the moment he pushed into him, his body instinctively clenching around the thick, unyielding stretch. A pleasured whine escaped before he could stop it, soft and broken as that familiar fire rushed back through him. It stole his breath, curled his toes, and dragged a tremble down his spine.

Zalith let out a low, guttural groan above him. "Fuck…you're always so tight, Alucard."

He barely heard him. His hands gripped the sheets, eyes fluttering shut as every nerve lit up again. His heat welcomed the intrusion greedily, and for a moment, it was almost too much. He tilted his head back, throat exposed, chest rising and falling in quiet gasps.

The demon leaned in again, one hand braced beside Alucard's head, the other still gripping his leg to keep him open. He started to move with slow, deep thrusts that made Alucard's mouth fall open in a silent moan and made his fingers curl hard into the bedding.

He sank into the pleasure like it was the only thing keeping him alive. He hooked his other leg around Zalith's waist, caging him in, pulling him deeper, harder. Every thrust punched a moan from his throat, ragged and desperate, and the heat inside him, already ravenous, flared hotter, devouring every last thread of thought.

Alucard couldn't think anymore. There was no shame, no self-doubt, no ache of inferiority, nothing but the pleasing drag of Zalith's dick inside him, and that overwhelming flood of sensation that left his body shaking and wet with pheromones. His back arched with each thrust, offering more, needing more, until he was moaning and wincing beneath the demon like he'd never catch his breath again.

Zalith's pace picked up, his breaths growing heavier, mouth open against Alucard's throat. He was close. Alucard could feel it in every tense muscle and staggered snap of his hips—and so was he. Again. The pressure twisted tight within him, rising fast, pulling him closer with every plunge.

The demon's thrusts turned rougher, his growls possessive against Alucard's neck. The bed jolted, every movement unrelenting—and then Zalith shuddered, his hips thrusting one final time as a pleasured cry tore from his throat, Alucard's name half spoken before breaking into another moan.

Alucard whined with him, the sudden burn and weight of his mate's cum sending him over the edge. Pleasure exploded through him; his back arched again, muscles drawn tight as a pleasured gasp left him, his own orgasm tearing free in pulses that left his body trembling, his mind blank. The haze of heat dulled, just for a moment, overtaken by the crashing wave of euphoria and the warm press of Zalith's body against his.

They stayed like that for a few moments, entwined and catching their breath. Zalith kissed him softly, again and again, dragging it out until their mouths were slow and swollen and the world had begun to settle around them.

Finally, the demon pulled back with a quiet, satisfied sound. He shifted off him carefully, one hand brushing along Alucard's thigh before he sat up and reached for the tissues on the bedside table. "Hold still," he murmured with a pleased little smile, already tending to the mess between them.

Zalith tossed the tissues aside and lay down beside him, his warmth immediately returning as he pulled Alucard close. One arm wrapped around his waist, anchoring him there, and the other slipped beneath his head. Their bodies fit together seamlessly, skin to skin, heartbeat to heartbeat.

Alucard melted into it at first. The heat of Zalith's chest against his back soothed the ache in his limbs, and the steady rhythm of his mate's breathing made the world feel safe again. He let himself be held, closing his eyes, his muscles softening one by one as he listened to the silence that followed.

But the quiet didn't last. Not in his mind.

The warmth that had blanketed him began to thin, replaced by the creeping edge of thought, the echo of his own body giving out too soon. He couldn't stop thinking about the way Zalith had taken over, the way he always seemed to be the one bringing Alucard to the edge—*effortlessly*.

He swallowed hard, and his fingers curled slightly against Zalith's arm. Was his mate disappointed? Did he wish he could give him more, that he could last longer, stay in control, and do what a man *should* be able to do?

His chest tightened. The thought didn't creep in, it *pierced* like a talon. That bitter sting of inadequacy wound tighter with every breath, curling coldly beneath his ribs. He'd tried more times than he wanted to admit since they'd left Atheson nearly two weeks ago; he'd tried to prove that he was enough, that he could take charge and fuck Zalith the way he was supposed to. But he failed *every single time*. His body betrayed him, claimed by heat too fast and eager. It didn't matter how much he wanted to give or how much he *meant* to give. It never worked.

Because he wasn't made right, was he?

His body looked the part most days. Broad shoulders, flat chest, strong jaw; the stubble helped, though he could only tolerate it for so long. But beneath the surface, beneath the illusion he'd fought to maintain, there was always that doubt and confusion…that wrongness, a body that didn't quite line up with the man he claimed to be.

He wanted to believe he *was* a man. He *was*. He'd chosen it—though he still didn't know when or why or how. But still, he'd lived it and fought for it. However, moments like this stripped that confidence down to the bone…because if he really was one, fully and truly, shouldn't he be able to *do this*?

And would a man really feel the desperation to carry his mate's child the way his heat made him?

No.

Instead, he felt like a ghost of a man, wearing something close to masculinity like a borrowed skin, close enough to pretend, but never close enough to believe.

He closed his eyes, and shame prickled across his skin. He hated this—he hated *himself* like this. And yet, the sting didn't fade. It bloomed painfully and silently, and he lay still in Zalith's arms, drowning in it.

What he'd remembered last night only added to the despair. He remembered how the priestesses forced him to stand alone; he wasn't like every other child trapped in those catacombs, and they all thought the same thing—that he was strange, that he was disgusting, that he was some kind of freak. No matter what the situation had been, those priestesses and the other children never looked at him as anything more than an abomination.

The demon dragged his tongue up the curve of Alucard's neck, groaning quietly against his skin. "There's nothing I love more than fucking you before the day starts," he murmured and sank his teeth lightly into his ear, making the vampire flinch. He growled low, wrapping his arms around him like a vice, nipping his lobe. "It marks you," he breathed, his voice thick with hunger. He licked his neck again. "My scent all over you, my cum buried so deep inside you *all day*…so everyone knows you're mine."

Alucard smiled a little. Zalith's possessiveness always sent a shiver through him no matter how overbearing his thoughts were. "I like vhen you mark me," he said, trying to focus on his mate.

Zalith licked up the side of his neck *again*. "I could keep marking you until the sun sets," he growled.

The words struck deep. Alucard's instincts flared, urging him to surrender again, to *beg* and forget everything else, to drown in the gnawing, relentless desire. And he wanted to. He wanted Zalith's hands, his mouth, his body, his *dick*—anything to silence the doubt clawing through his chest. But he knew how it would end. The euphoria never lasted. Every time Zalith so easily wrung pleasure from him, it chipped away at something inside, reminding him that no matter how badly he wanted to be enough, he wasn't.

Still, he turned to face his mate, summoning a smile when their eyes met. Zalith's smirk was devastating, all fangs and charm and confidence. And when their mouths collided, Alucard let himself sink. The slide of their tongues, the press of their lips, the warmth of Zalith's body, and the slow build of desire—it all helped blur the edges of his self-loathing just for a while…just long enough.

Maybe the guilt would come later. Maybe the dysphoria would roar louder than ever. But right now, he wanted something else to feel.

So he pulled Zalith over him, dragging him close by the hips, and the demon straddled his lap without hesitation. Their kisses turned avid, hands tangling in hair and clutching at bare skin, and the fire between them reignited in a shared moan.

And then—

Thump.

They both froze.

Another thump, followed by the rattle of claws on glass.

Zalith slowly turned his head towards the window, brows lifting in irritated disbelief, and Alucard looked, too. An owl sat perched on the ledge, large and pale-eyed, staring at them through the tiny crack in the curtains. A scroll was tied around one of its legs, sealed in dark crimson wax.

Alucard groaned and let his head fall back against the pillow. This time, though…he was almost glad of the interruption. He wanted Zalith—he *always* wanted him—but the dysphoria was worsening by the day, and pretty soon, he knew he'd be drowning so violently that he wouldn't be able to come up for any more breaths of air.

"Is probably an update vrom Mărioara and Gheorghiţă. Is Saturday, avter all."

"Right," Zalith said, clearly having needed a moment to recall what day it was.

Alucard didn't blame him; he knew how lost his mate became in his scent. If it were any other message, he'd ignore it for now, but he was waiting for updates on Aegis activity. He still needed to pick a target.

The vampire got out of bed and pulled his trousers on. He headed over to the window, opened it, and took the message from the owl.

"Come back here," Zalith complained, pouting.

He smiled and joined the demon in bed again, cuddling up to him. As Zalith nuzzled against his neck, Alucard unrolled the paper. It *was* from Mărioara and Gheorghiţă. A few more Aegis had turned up, and he should both add them to the map he'd been working on *and* consider whether or not one of them could be his target.

As he stroked his fingers down Zalith's arm, he said, "I 'ave to go and update zhe map."

Zalith growled quietly. "No," he murmured.

"Zhe sooner I do, zhe sooner ve can lie down again."

The demon groaned.

"And vhile I get started, *you* can go and get me some 'ot chocolate," he said firmly.

Zalith smiled against his neck. "Yes, sir," he said with a sultry hum.

Alucard lingered a moment longer, rolling the paper closed. He let himself sink into his mate's warmth…just for a breath, but he knew better than to stay. The longer he lay there, the greater the chance that dismay would creep back in.

So he sat up. "Come on," he said quietly.

Zalith grunted in protest but followed, stretching as he rose.

They dressed slowly, each movement heavy with the weight of restraint. Alucard struggled not to glance back at the bed, not to surrender to the comfort that still clung to the sheets. But he didn't. He led them downstairs, the pull of purpose just strong enough to anchor him.

There was an Aegis to hunt.

And a darker part of himself that he was still trying to outrun.

Chapter Four

— ⟨ † ⟩ —

Prepare

| **Alucard** |
| *Uzlia Isles, Usrul, Castle Reiner* |

The thick oak doors closed behind Alucard with a dull thud as he stepped into the war room. Every sound outside was muted, leaving only the quiet hum of enchanted weapons and wards. Dimly lit hanging lanterns were the only light source, protecting moon-enchanted blades from sunlight. Dark mahogany panels lined the walls, interrupted only by weapons mounted with militant pride: sabres, revolvers, long-range rifles with inlaid gold filigree, and newer Arcana firearms with crystal cartridges and exposed conduits that pulsed faintly with stored ethos.

He moved towards the centre of the room, the soft fur rug a relief to his feet—he hated how cold the marble floor could get. The war table dominated the space, a massive slab of black-stained ironwood rimmed with brass, the world map carved into its surface with the astonishing detail he'd been *very* adamant about when he'd commissioned it a century ago. Dozens of small, golden dragon statues were placed across the continents, their gilded wings and sharpened claws gleaming in the light, some solid gold while others had black trims; each had a name carved into the rim of the circular bases. Some stood alone, others in clusters, marking the locations of every currently known Aegis. Alucard trailed his fingers across the edge of the table, glancing around the room again. He and Zalith had been preparing for every possible outcome.

Shelves brimmed with tactical ledgers and leather-bound logs stood around the room's edges, along with crystal communicators set in claw-like metal stands and scrolls sealed with coloured wax. In one corner sat a locked iron case lined with ebonsteel, containing classified relics too dangerous to leave unguarded—blades that drank ethos, vials of cursed blood, even a demonbone dagger that Zalith had obtained decades ago.

He shifted his full attention to the table and unrolled Mărioara and Gheorghiţă's message again. As he read, he repositioned several dragon pieces, and then he took four more from the table drawer beneath him and placed them on the map.

Erysa was no longer in Avalmoor or Aegisguard altogether. He took her piece off the map.

Asul had moved from Odessius to Ascela. He slid his piece to the new location.

Adenaver had left the world, too.

Molgaruun, Khalidrax, Aurexion, and Velmorrak had appeared, two in Avalmoor and the other two in Nophia. He moved their black-trimmed statues along the table and exhaled deeply, tapping his chin. The four of them were among the eighteen of Letholdus' demi-gods, much more dangerous than the lesser Aegis.

The door then opened. He took his eyes off the map and watched as Zalith closed the door and walked towards him with two white mugs—one filled with coffee, and the other with hot chocolate, as Alucard had requested.

"Here, baby." The demon smiled at him, handing him his hot chocolate.

"Vank you," he said, and as he took it, Zalith kissed his cheek.

Zalith stood beside him and looked down at the map. "So, what's been updated?"

"Zhe vhree I mentioned vhen ve vere in Maluhia 'ave changed position. Erysa and Adenaver 'ave levt zhe vorld, and Asul is in Ascela. Considering 'ow many Aegis' are zhere vight now, I vink zhat ve should avoid zhat place."

"Agreed. Who else can you get the fur from?"

"Kovrier is in Sinéad vight now," he started, pointing to each Aegis' statue. "Dadrid is in Tái Qián…and Niedreid 'as been seen in Divinos. Zhey are vhree of zhe veakest Aegis, but zhey're all var avay. Gydrucrit is in Akhir—zhat's just beyond DeiganLupus, but 'e is dangerous. And zhen Ondrilth is in Avalmoor vith Uvoilun—zhey are not *zhat* dangerous on zheir own, but togezzer, zhey might be a challenge," he explained, glancing at Zalith. "Vhich vone should ve go vor? Zhe closest or zhe least dangerous?"

"The least dangerous," he instantly answered. "I don't want you getting hurt."

Alucard nodded. "Vell…Dadrid possesses ethos zhat allows 'im to manipulate zhe earth avound 'im, but 'e's in Tái Qián, vhich is very mountainous, so ve'd best not go zhere. Gydrucrit is in Akhir, a small island; 'e can manipulate light, so if ve vent later, ve could get zhere vor dusk, and 'e vouldn't 'ave much light to use. Or Niedreid is in Divinos—she is…vire dragon," he said, pointing to Divinos on the map. "Is close enough vor me to vly us zhere."

"Will you have enough energy to fight her after that, though?" he asked worriedly.

The vampire smiled. "I'll be vine. I 'ave you to 'elp me."

"Last time I was near a dragon, I almost died," he said with a small laugh. "But I'll do my best."

Alucard placed his hot chocolate on the table and placed his hands on Zalith's waist, pulling him closer. "Vell, last time, ve veren't prepared. But *zhis* time, ve know vhat ve are dealing vith."

"And what are we dealing with, vampire?"

"Niedreid is small drake with vire ethos. Ve both 'ave our own vire, so ve'll be vine."

"Cakewalk," Zalith said with a smirk.

Alucard smiled and looked down at the map as he picked up his hot chocolate and took a few sips. "Ve should make plan. Drakes are small; zhey may not 'ave vings, but zhey make up vor zhat vith zheir agility—zhey are very vast," he explained.

Zalith nodded, placing his coffee on the table.

"Zhey can control zheir vire a lot more zhan a dragon—zhey can…make move vherever and 'owever zhey vant."

The demon moved his hand down Alucard's back, nodding as he listened.

Alucard frowned, glancing at him. "All drakes 'ave zhe ability to disorientate and deaven zheir opponents vith a single roar, so ve should make our virst priority to take out zhe little vocal cord in 'er neck zhat lets 'er do zhat."

Zalith nodded, moving his hand down to Alucard's ass—

The vampire snatched Zalith's wrist and glared at him as he smiled innocently.

"What?" he asked, laughing.

"Ve need to be serious," he answered. "Drakes are dangerous."

"I know. I'm taking it very seriously," Zalith said, smiling.

Pouting, Alucard let go of his wrist and looked back down at the map. "Divinos is a very densely populated country. Zhere is a lot of jungle and vorests—a lot of vildlife zhat vill try to eat us if ve zon't pay attention," he said sternly.

"Like what?" his mate asked, still smiling.

Alucard turned to face him and leaned on the desk. "Snakes zhe size of boats, six-legged cats zhe size of 'orses. Zhere are many kinds of lycans out zhere, too. Not to mention zhe vizards zhat live zhere."

"Lizards?"

"No…" he grumbled. "Vizards."

"Oh," Zalith said, teasing him.

The vampire gestured to the map. "My scouts 'ave said Niedreid is in zhe Eastern Mountains—zhere's a cave at zhe base of zhe mountain vith Ephriel carved into."

A repulsed look appeared on Zalith's face. "Ew," he mumbled, moving his hand down Alucard's back once again. "What's the terrain like?" he asked, slowly untucking the vampire's shirt.

As Zalith moved his hand under his shirt and started dragging his fingers over his skin, the vampire pouted and tried to concentrate. "Is mostly vlat land, veally tall trees, mountains to zhe east and south. Vains a lot, too."

"Do you think the dragon will be in the cave?"

"She 'as been seen coming in and out of zhere—zhe locals say zhe Aegis guards a 'great treasure'," he mumbled. "I zon't know vhat's in zhere or if is true."

"Is it worth looking into?"

Alucard shrugged. "Could be."

Zalith's hand slipped around from Alucard's back, his palm warm as it smoothed over the ridges of his abdomen, pausing just below his ribs before trailing lower.

A shiver coiled up Alucard's spine, unwelcome and electric. Heat pooled fast inside him, instinct crackling just beneath the surface like flint waiting for a spark. But he clung to focus. "Zhe Aegis 'ave alvays guarded vhat's sacred to zhem. Or to zhe Numen," he managed, though his voice dipped.

Zalith's lips curled into a slow smirk. "Should we go ourselves…or send others in first?" he asked, fingers slipping just beneath the edge of Alucard's belt.

It was a cruel distraction. Every brush of skin made it harder to think, to stay in the moment. His heat was bad enough on its own, pulsing through him in steady waves, but this…this was Zalith's touch. It was familiar and claiming, always just one step from undoing him completely.

He pulled in a shallow breath, his body traitorously arching towards more. It didn't matter how many times he told himself to resist, or that this wasn't the time. The craving was still there, growing and gnawing as if his instincts knew exactly what buttons to press to eclipse his doubt and drag him under.

Still, the hesitation clung to him like fog. He hated how easily he could be tipped off-balance, how the smallest act could unearth thoughts he'd tried so hard to bury. He wasn't weak, but something inside him whispered otherwise. A quiet, insidious voice that never quite shut up; that old sense of not being right, of not fitting the body he was in or the role he was supposed to fill…it crept back up his throat like bile.

He tried not to think about it. He tried to focus on the mission, the map, the threat, anything but the way Zalith's hand lingered, coaxing and patient, tempting him to abandon the pretence of control…because if he didn't push back soon, he knew he'd give in—just like always.

"Ve can…look ourselves vonce ve get zhere," Alucard said, forcing his voice steady as he pushed the thoughts away.

"Okay," Zalith murmured, his hand drifting down towards Alucard's crotch.

But Alucard caught his wrist mid-motion. His grip wasn't hard, but the reluctance in it spoke volumes. "Not vight now," he said quietly, avoiding his gaze.

Zalith's smile was gentle. "Yes, sir," he said amusedly, withdrawing his hand without argument. He closed the space between them instead, pressing in close and nuzzling the side of Alucard's face.

The vampire didn't move at first. He just stood there, jaw clenched, skin prickling with the aftershocks of tension that had nowhere to go. Then he shifted, meaning to face the table, but the motion made his shirt ride up slightly, baring a strip of his lower stomach. Zalith's hand brushed it on instinct, and the touch was casual, fleeting.

But it was enough.

Alucard flinched—not from pain but from the sudden wave of self-loathing that surged up at the feel of his own skin, too soft, not what it *was supposed* to be. He pulled away with a sigh, smoothing the fabric back down like that would help, and turned his focus to the map instead. "Vill take vour hours to vly to Divinos," he said. "Vhen do you vant to leave?" He glanced sideways but didn't meet Zalith's eyes.

Zalith let out a low, sultry laugh and pressed a kiss to Alucard's cheek. "Mm…four whole hours of being entirely inside each other."

Alucard was halfway to a retort—that wasn't how he'd put it—but he hesitated. Zalith wasn't exactly wrong. When they dematerialized into smoke, their forms *did* blend, coiling into one another, weightless and fused. Technically…yes.

Still. *Why was he thinking about that?*

He exhaled. "I—"

"I wish I could fuck you like that," Zalith groaned against his neck, his voice rough with desire. "Be inside you in every way."

The words sent a pulse of heat through him, but they also struck something deeper— something more fragile. He didn't reply right away. He just stood there, heart thudding, letting Zalith's breath warm his throat, trying to hold on to that thread of intimacy before the self-doubt unravelled it.

"Can you still feel my cum inside you?" the demon whispered.

Alucard's breath caught. He swallowed, his hand tightening on the edge of the table as heat surged low in his stomach, uninvited and overpowering. "Yes," he said, the word slipping out quieter than he intended. And he *could*. The warmth deep inside him hadn't faded entirely, not with his heat still burning through his veins. He could feel the faint, slick fullness when he shifted his stance, like his body had held onto it on purpose, like it *wanted* to be claimed and owned.

Zalith moved behind him, not quite touching but close enough that Alucard could feel the energy of his gaze. "Still aching?" he asked, voice low and coaxing.

The vampire closed his eyes for a second. "Yes."

"Still stretched open for me?"

A shiver rolled down his spine, and a wave of arousal crashed through him. When Zalith reached out and brushed his hand down his side, he nearly winced.

"Good," the demon murmured, his palm flattening against his hip. "I hope you never stop feeling it."

Alucard bit his lip. He wanted to say something sharp, to act like he still had control, but it was gone, melting beneath the growing pressure in his gut. His body was already responding, already hardening. The dysphoria hadn't vanished, but it had been pushed back by the haze, by that familiar, inescapable craving for more.

He tilted his head back, inviting Zalith closer

The demon didn't hesitate. His lips brushed Alucard's throat first, and then pressed lower, dragging a kiss over the hollow of his neck as his hands gripped Alucard's waist and pulled him flush against him. Their bodies slid together effortlessly, heat to heat, hardness against hardness, the pressure delicious and maddening.

Zalith kissed him, deep and slow, the kind that stole thought and replaced it with hunger. Alucard gave in with a soft sound, his hands sliding up to Zalith's chest, clinging. Their hips rocked once, again, and the friction sent a jolt through him.

"Mmm," Zalith growled, low and pleased against his mouth. One hand slipped between them and palmed him through his trousers. "You're already leaking for me," he whispered, dragging his knuckles along the front of Alucard's bulge, catching the damp spot spreading through the fabric. "So eager. You always are, even when you pretend you're not."

Alucard flushed, the heat of it clashing with the heady desire. He didn't want to think—not about himself, his body, or the things he didn't like about it. But the sensation and the praise…the *attention*—it was all beginning to spin out into something vulnerable.

Zalith pressed another kiss to his mouth and then moved to his jaw, trailing slow, open-mouthed kisses towards his ear. "Do you want more?"

Alucard nodded before he could stop himself.

But as Zalith's hand moved to undo his trousers, that awful, slithering doubt began creeping back in, threading through the pleasure like rot. He was the one making Alucard fall apart again. He always did. And *him*? What did he give Zalith?

His fingers hesitated against Zalith's chest. He turned his face slightly, not quite pulling away, but no longer giving in either. That familiar ache, the one that had nothing to do with heat, tightened in his chest.

"Vait," he murmured.

Zalith stopped stroking his bulge but kept nuzzling his neck. "What's wrong?"

"Noving," he said, trying to sound as if that were true. "Ve should start getting veady. I zon't vant to visk Niedreid leaving Divinos."

The demon groaned quietly. "You know I can make you cum in less than a minute," he murmured, starting to stroke his crotch again. "A minute won't hurt, will it?"

That made him feel worse. "I just vant to get zhis over vith," he said, turning away from him.

"Okay," Zalith said, sounding confused. But then he sighed softly. "I'm sorry."

He shook his head. "Is okay."

"It's just…maddening," the demon mumbled, resting his chin on Alucard's shoulder and wrapping his arms around him.

Alucard could feel the demon's hard length pressing against his leg. The fact that he knew it wasn't an intentional tease made the anticipation much more intense, but he did his best to fight it…and everything else that tried crawling into his mind.

"Ve'll need some vings," he said, finishing his hot chocolate.

Zalith placed his empty mug on the table. "What do we need?"

Alucard made his way over to one of the cabinets. "Severium," he answered, carefully sorting through several small glass boxes, each of which contained differently shaped and coloured crystals. "Contains gold, vemember? Gold negates an Aegis' sensory abilities and is also very vlammable vhen zemon vire is applied. Vill be usevul against Niedreid."

The demon smiled as Alucard glanced over his shoulder at him. "Oh, yeah. I remember."

Once he located the box of white, wand-shaped crystals, Alucard carefully removed it from the cabinet and stared down at the contents. Gold streaks veined through the pale wands like molten rivers, shimmering faintly beneath the surface. Severium was so beautiful but so lethal.

"Ve can use zhese to disorientate 'er," he murmured, setting the box gently on the table beside him. Then he reached up to a shelf and grabbed a handful of black revolver rounds from a worn tin box. "And zhese," he continued, holding them up between his fingers, "zhese vill shut down 'er ethos vonce zhe poison inside gets into her blood." He loaded the bullets into one of his gold colts and then turned and held the weapon out to Zalith, handle-first. "Zhis is for you."

"Me?" Zalith asked, laughing almost nervously.

He nodded. "Is…extra precaution," he insisted.

Zalith looked down at the gun and then at Alucard again.

"You can't use your ethos against an Aegis—vell…your vire vould vork, but zhat's about all. I can use luciverium, you vill use zhat," he said, placing the gun in Zalith's hand. "I vill teach you 'ow to shoot."

"Good," Zalith said. "Because I'm going to need practice."

Alucard nodded. "Ve can go outside," he said, picking up the box of severium *and* his other colt.

"Thank you," Zalith said with a smile, walking alongside Alucard as they made their way towards the front door. After a beat, he added quietly, "What if I'm terrible at it?"

Alucard grabbed and pulled on his coat, and then he pushed open the door and stepped into the courtyard, the cold air brushing against his face. "You'll be vine—is simple, veally."

"Okay," he murmured, though his voice carried more doubt than certainty.

The vampire glanced back at him with a small, reassuring smile and led the way down the stone steps into one of the lower gardens. He stopped near a crumbling wall and turned to face him. "You vill be vine," he said again, firmer this time. He reached for the gold colt Zalith carried and exchanged it for his other—this one loaded with standard rounds. "Zhe black vounds are mine. Vhen I use zhem, I vely on my sensory ethos to guide my aim. Try to do zhe same." He plucked an apple from a basket beside the wall and set it atop the stone ledge. Then, taking Zalith's free hand, he led him about twenty feet away before stepping aside. "Just aim for zhe apple," he said, nodding at the distant red dot. "Vocus. Let your ethos do zhe vest. You von't miss."

Zalith eyed the colt in his hand, and then he turned to Alucard with a playful smile. "How do I hold it?" he asked amusedly.

Alucard wasn't surprised—of course Zalith hadn't ever handled a firearm before. Demons didn't need them. He returned the smile and stepped in close again, placing his hand gently over Zalith's. "Like zhis," he murmured, guiding the demon's fingers. He adjusted Zalith's grip, ensuring his palm sat firmly against the backstrap, then raised his arm so the barrel pointed directly at the apple. "Vinger goes 'ere," he added, nudging Zalith's index finger lightly against the trigger guard before settling it on the trigger.

Zalith's smirk only widened.

The vampire continued, sliding Zalith's thumb into place. "Zhis is zhe 'ammer— you'll need to cock zhis back bevore every shot," he explained, pulling it down until it clicked. "Zhis colt is single-action, so each shot takes prep. And zhere vill be vecoil, so keep your arm steady—brace your vrist a little."

Zalith nodded, but the glint in his eyes said he wasn't just listening. "Got it," he said, his voice low, "pull, steady, aim…and try not to get distracted by my instructor."

Alucard pouted and stepped back. "Veady?" he asked, folding his arms with a tilt of his head.

The demon gave a nod, and then he turned his attention from Alucard to the apple perched on the wall. He raised the colt, took a breath, and aimed.

Alucard watched in silence, arms folded, gaze sharp.

A split second later, the shot rang out—loud and sharp. The bullet struck the apple dead-on, sending it bursting apart in a splatter of pulp before what remained thudded into the grass behind the wall.

"*Foarte bine*," Alucard said with a pleased smile, giving a small, approving clap. "See? I told you—is simple." He stepped forward again as Zalith lowered the colt.

Zalith grinned, switching the colt to his left hand before wrapping his right arm around Alucard's shoulders and pulling him into a loose, satisfied hug. "I had a good teacher," he murmured, nuzzling close. "And I like it when you speak to me in Dor-Sanguian," he added, smirking against Alucard's cheek.

Alucard smiled and kissed Zalith's cheek. "*Te iubesc.*"

"What did you say?" Zalith asked with a curious smile.

The vampire laughed a little. "I love you."

"Aw, I love you too," he said and kissed Alucard's lips.

With a content smile, Alucard rested his forehead against Zalith's. But the moment he saw that seductive little smile on the demon's lips, he asked, "Do you vant to practice more, or should ve get veady to go?"

"*Should* I practice more?"

"Yes," Alucard answered. "Zhere are still vive more vounds in zhat barrel," he said, nodding down at the colt in Zalith's hand. "I zon't 'ave any more apples on me, but…you can shoot zhose vones off zhat tree," he said, pointing to one of the many apple trees in the garden. "Vhile you do zhat, I vill go and get everyving else ve need."

"Okay," Zalith said and kissed him again.

Alucard left Zalith to practise and made his way back into the castle. In the war room, he crossed to one of the weapon cabinets and retrieved two revolver holsters—one for himself and one for Zalith; each was already stocked with several reloads' worth of rounds. He grabbed an additional handful of ammunition, slipping it into his coat pocket before slinging the holsters over his shoulder. Finally, he took a golden ring from the box full of golden jewellery next to the map-stacked shelf, and then he headed out.

On his way through the entrance hall, he paused at the coatrack beside the door. He pulled on his leather gloves, easing his claws through the fingertip slits, and threw his fur-collared cape over his shoulders, fastening it at the neck. Then he reached for his cane, the elegant black shaft concealing the sword within, and finally plucked Zalith's coat from the hook.

By the time he stepped back into the garden, five clean shots had already rung out from the far end. Zalith stood near the wall, lowering the colt with a satisfied look as he spotted Alucard approaching, eyes bright beneath the lingering scent of gunpowder.

Seeing that Zalith had successfully shot five apples from the tree, Alucard smiled. "You got zhe 'ang of zhat pretty quickly," he said, stopping in front of him.

"Thank you," Zalith said with a smile. "And thank you for the coat," he added as Alucard handed it to him.

Alucard returned the smile with a nod as Zalith passed him the now-empty colt. "If you're veady, ve can go now," he said, but instead of holstering the weapon immediately, he paused. "'Ere," he murmured, thumbing open the revolver's cylinder. He showed Zalith how to eject the spent shells, then loaded six fresh rounds from his pocket. "Push zhis to velease," he explained, "and turn zhis like so to votate. You'll get vaster vith practice."

Zalith watched with rapt attention, clearly fascinated. "You really know your way around these," he said with a small grin.

Alucard smirked faintly and drew one of the holsters from over his shoulder. "Zhis is for you." He stepped closer and secured it around Zalith's waist, adjusting the strap and checking the fit before tightening the buckle. "Is alveady loaded vith spare vounds," he added, patting the row of gleaming brass nestled in the leather.

Zalith looked down at it and then up at him with a wider grin. "I like it," he said, clearly pleased. "You make it look so effortless."

"Because *is*," Alucard replied, but there was warmth in his voice as he turned to finally secure his own colt in its holster. "Oh, and zhis," he added, holding out the golden ring. "To stop zhe Aegis vrom detecting you."

The demon said, "Thank you," as he took it for him. But he didn't put it on straight away. He looked at Alucard's hand, smiled, and said, "Here."

He took Alucard's steel ring from his right index finger and moved it to his ring finger, and then he did the same with his own. Then, he put the gold ring on his index finger. "So we're still matching; I think they look better this way."

He was right. "Zhey do," he agreed.

Zalith kissed his lips.

After another smile at him, Alucard asked, "Are you veady?"

The demon nodded once. "I'm ready."

Alucard wrapped his arms around his mate, and without delay, he dematerialized them both into vermillion smoke and raced up into the sky, heading for Divinos.

Chapter Five

Divinos

| **Zalith** |

| *The Vorynthian Ocean* |

As they drifted through the gloomy skies, Zalith cast his gaze sideways. The vast ocean stretched endlessly beneath them, its surface dull and dappled with the reflection of clouds that swelled like bruises in the sky. The wind passed through their smoke-like form without resistance, carrying with it the faint scent of sea salt and distance. It was oddly quiet, just the hush of air and the weight of thoughts pressing in.

He looked up, once again seeing what he always saw when Alucard flew with him like this. Four wings eerily slicing in and out of the smoke, a long, serpentine tail coiling like shadowed silk through the air. Zalith blinked, trying to anchor the vision, but the smoke always seemed to hide just enough. Only one thing shone clearly: his fiancé's hell-lit eyes glowing through the red fog like furnaces left half-shuttered.

What *was* he?

Zalith glanced down at himself, but unlike Alucard's form—however veiled—his own offered no shape, no anchor. Just vermillion haze drifting in rhythm with the flight. He felt himself there, but there was no body to observe. Alucard, though… Alucard was something *else*. Something ancient. Something powerful.

He never got the chance to ask about it… but was now the time? They had an Aegis to find and kill. A grounded dragon, older than most ageless beings. He'd memorized Alucard's briefings, learned to shoot a colt, and told himself over and over that he was ready. But even now, he could still smell the vampire's pheromones, even in this form, even *here*.

The memory of earlier temptation pressed into him like heat. He knew Alucard had turned him down not out of disinterest, but it was still hard. His mate was in heat. Zalith was so close he could almost taste him on the air, yet he couldn't do anything about it.

He clenched his focus tightly around the mission. There would be time for sex once the drake was dead.

But his instincts refused to listen to sense.

With a huff, he focused, grasping onto his and Alucard's imprint connection. *"Alucard?"* he asked, speaking into his mind.

"Yes?" his vampire answered.

"Inside this smoke, are you in your true form?"

He didn't immediately reply. When he said, *"I'm not sure,"* he sounded confused.

It made sense, though. Why would he have seen his reflection in this form? *"Haven't you ever been curious?"*

"Not veally."

Zalith laughed amusedly. *"Really? You haven't thought about turning to smoke in front of a very big mirror?"*

"No."

"Sure," he said doubtfully.

"I 'aven't."

"I don't believe you."

"I just… look like smoke," he grumbled.

"You look like a lizard."

"I'm not lizard."

"You look like one."

"No, I zon't."

"I've seen your true form, vampire. You're a lizard," he teased him.

"Vhatever," he muttered, clearly pouting.

He laughed again. *"I'm just messing with you."*

A quiet grumble came in response.

"You're lucky we're all misty right now or I'd be kissing your cute little face."

"And licking, too."

"Especially licking it." His curiosity returned. *"Can I really not touch you while we're like this?"*

"No. Ve're not technically vhysical at all. Ve're just enigma."

"So… this isn't like the smoke that vampires turn into?"

"Zhey become actual smoke. I am smoke… and somesing else. And vampires can't transport ozzer vings or people vith zhem."

He was *still* learning, and he loved it. *"Everything about you fascinates me, Alucard,"* he said, more a compliment than a flirt.

"You vascinate me, too," he replied, sounding content.

Zalith wanted to flirt *now*, but he held back. They'd be in Divinos soon, and he had to make sure that both he and Alucard were focused and ready. He'd give in to his instincts later.

↤ ❖ ↦

| *Saen-Jirra, Divinos, Kulogdan, Tigsalanta Territory* |

Divinos was unlike anywhere Zalith had ever seen.

At first, it felt like they'd only been travelling for twenty minutes; adrift in the calm haze of ethos-smoke, time had slipped by without weight. But when Zalith checked his pocket watch, a flicker of surprise crossed his face. Nearly four hours had passed.

They emerged on a stretch of white sand so fine that it shimmered like crushed pearls. The sea at their backs was impossibly clear, casting ribbons of turquoise light that danced over the shoreline with every gentle wave, and the air was thick with warmth and humidity, fragrant with the scent of salt, orchids, and something sweet, almost like nectar.

Ahead, the beach gave way to an elegant jungle. Towering palms arched overhead, their fronds trailing like veils in the sun-dappled breeze. Massive moss-covered roots twisted over the undergrowth, while vines hung like green silk from the canopy. The calls of strange birds and distant animals echoed through the trees, almost like musical notes that seemed to harmonize with the faint, chiming hum of ethos…because the land was Arcanean. Zalith could feel it beneath his feet; it brushed against his skin, and it lingered in the very air that he breathed.

Veins of glowing blue crystal jutted from between roots and stone, pulsing faintly with soft shades of blue, violet, and gold; some seemed to hum, and others cracked faintly in the heat as if holding something volatile within. The light from them bounced against the canopy, casting reflections that shimmered on the leaves like fireflies made of glass.

Zalith took a step forward and stared in quiet wonder, soaking it in—the colour, the sounds, the fragrant, glittering air. "It's beautiful," he murmured, mostly to himself as he tried to settle the strange sense that the land itself was watching. He couldn't tell whether it was welcoming or warning them, but considering what they were here for, he strongly suspected that it was the latter.

Alucard smiled at him. "Is just as I vemember."

"I was expecting something…ominous," he said with a smirk. "Because dragons are kind of…ominous."

"Kind of veminds me of vhere ve vent vor our little vacation," the vampire said, taking hold of Zalith's hand.

"It does," he agreed. "You better not find any stray animals to bring home."

"I von't," Alucard mumbled, starting to lead the way along the beach.

Zalith smiled, walking at his side. "I suppose I'll believe it when I don't see it."

"Ve are 'ere vor business," he said as they walked into the palm tree forest. "Zhere's no time to go searching vor animals."

"You have a way of finding them even when you aren't searching."

Alucard pouted. "No, I zon't."

"Tell that to the turtle—and those cats you found."

The vampire frowned—

"And Sabazios."

As the palm tree forest became a jungle, Alucard sighed quietly. "Vhatever," he grumbled. "Is not my vault zhat zhey all so 'appen to cross my path."

"If I were a stray cat, I'd do the same thing," he said, smirking a little.

Alucard shrugged. "Vell, you *vere* a stray zemon who so 'appened to cross my path, and now, 'ere ve are," he said, returning his smirk.

"Do you make out with all your pets, too?"

He pouted and scowled. "No."

The demon laughed amusedly.

And then they went quiet, leaving only the sounds of the forest.

Of course, the first thing that consumed Zalith was instinct. The pull towards Alucard was immediate, like gravity thickened by the heat still radiating from him. Even now, with the filtered sunlight catching in his hair and the scent of orchids clinging to his coat, Alucard seemed made to distract him. So Zalith moved closer, his steps unconsciously syncing with his mate's as they pushed through a narrow tangle of roots and vine-laced underbrush.

But as soon as he got near enough to feel the warmth trailing off the vampire's skin, something tugged him out of the haze.

Alucard had hesitated this morning.

Zalith frowned slightly. They had a mission to do, yes, but this wasn't like before. This wasn't a time-sensitive sprint against a ruthless hunter or a city in peril. It felt like they had time. Zalith had thought…well, he'd thought Alucard would've wanted him just as much as always. Especially now. Especially in heat.

But maybe that was the problem.

He ducked beneath a low-hanging branch. The forest was dense with sound—chirping insects, the distant trill of tropical birds, and the hum of unseen ethos laced through the leaves and soil. Crystals jutting from the mossy ground refracted the sunlight and sent flickers of colour dancing across Alucard's back. The beauty of it all should have filled him with wonder, and part of him *did* admire it—the rich, humid scent of wet bark and nectar, the towering canopy overhead—but another part of him was caught up in the silence between them.

Had he pushed too hard? Had he ignored something Alucard wasn't saying? Or had he not paid enough attention to something his mate had already said?

"Alucard?" he asked.

The vampire looked at him.

"Why didn't you want to have sex with me earlier?"

Alucard frowned, seeming almost startled by his question. "Vhat?"

He didn't want to be too serious about it—the last thing he wanted was to make his vampire feel pressured or uncomfortable. Alucard didn't need a reason not to want sex, and Zalith didn't expect an explanation; he was just…curious. Maybe a little worried, too. So he asked, "Is it because I can't kiss like Peaches can?"

Still frowning, Alucard shrugged a little. "No…I just…zidn't veel like earlier."

"Why not? Should I try different moves?" he asked with a smirk.

The vampire shook his head and sighed sullenly. "I vas just vocused on getting veady to come out 'ere and vind Niedreid."

Was that really why? He wasn't going to push. "Okay," he said.

Alucard frowned in confliction and looked at him. "Are you…mad?"

"No," Zalith answered, staring ahead. "I'm just a little confused—but not mad."

"Vhy are you confused?"

He wouldn't lie to him, either. "Because normally, you don't say no, and your current biology suggests that you want to have sex. *And* this dragon hunt isn't necessarily a time-sensitive thing," he explained, moving a branch aside for him. "If you just didn't want to, that's okay, it just surprised me a little."

Alucard shrugged again, slowly staring down at the ground. "I'm sorry if I disappointed you. I zon't know, I just…zidn't veally veel like—even zhough I vant—is 'ard to explain," he mumbled with a shrug. "Maybe I'm tired. I zidn't sleep zhat great last night."

Zalith slid an arm around Alucard's waist and drew him in until their bodies pressed together, cloth and leather brushing softly between them. He pressed a gentle kiss against his cheek and offered a quiet smile. "It's okay," he murmured. "You don't have to explain. Don't worry about it."

They walked in silence for a while, the soft crunch of damp earth beneath their boots and the distant chatter of birds filling the humid air. Zalith tried to redirect his thoughts; he tried to focus on the mission, on the shifting scents of the rainforest or the lingering sweetness of Alucard's heat…but the knot in his chest only seemed to tighten.

It wasn't just confusion anymore. Something gnawed at him deeper than that.

Alucard had brushed him off this morning, and while Zalith hadn't pushed for an explanation or wanted to make it a thing, the moment kept echoing in his mind. Was he really just tired? Or was there more to it?

He frowned, staring at the path ahead, trying not to let the thought take root—but it did anyway.

Was he pulling away?

The idea twisted in his gut. He told himself it was nothing, that it didn't matter. But that wasn't true. He'd already lost so much lately; his people, his footing, his certainty. And now, without meaning to, he found himself wondering if this was the slow beginning of the end he dreaded.

Was Alucard growing bored of him? Tiring of the closeness? He didn't want to believe that. The vampire's hesitation had felt…guarded, not cold. But the doubt lingered.

He didn't want to ask, not when they had a mission to carry out. But the question was there now, lodged beneath his ribs like a splinter. And if it stayed, if it festered…he wasn't sure he'd be able to leave it alone for long.

Just then, Alucard veered off course with a sudden jolt, nearly stumbling. Zalith tensed. He didn't hesitate and followed, his instincts flaring as the vampire crossed to a nearby cluster of low-hanging shrubs. There was no warning, no explanation, and that alone made the demon uneasy. Was there danger ahead? A threat hidden just out of sight? Or—gods forbid—another wounded creature pulling his fiancé's heartstrings?

Either way, Zalith stayed close, senses sharpened and ready to strike if needed. "What is it?" he asked, watching as Alucard carefully reached into the thicket.

The vampire drew something from the tangled branches and lifted it slowly into view—a small tuft of glowing white fur, the fine strands laced with streaks of dull, drying blood. Even in the shade, it shimmered faintly, catching the light like spider silk.

"Zhis is vrom an Aegis," Alucard said, his voice low with tension. He turned the tuft between his fingers, frowning as he studied it. "Not a drake, zhough. A drake's vur is coarser. Zhis is…sovt. Like silk."

Zalith's stomach tightened. Something about the air had changed. He couldn't explain it, but it pressed against him like a weight, like the hush before a scream. "Should we leave?" he asked quietly.

Alucard shrugged. "I zon't know," he said, looking back at Zalith. "Zhis could be old. My scouts said zhe Aegis switched places just a vew days ago, so…zhis could belong to whoever vas 'ere bevore Niedreid."

"We should leave," Zalith decided. He didn't want to take any risks.

Alucard frowned, letting the fur fall from his fingers. "Are you sure? Ve came all zhis vay."

"I don't want you to get hurt," he said sadly, moving his hand over Alucard's shoulder.

"I von't," he said firmly. "Zhis is vhat I vas meant to do, avter all. And ve are both prepared vor anyving—ve 'ave each ozzer's backs, no?" he added, smirking.

Zalith's hesitation didn't fade. "I just…don't want to lose you," he said quietly, his worry intensifying.

The vampire moved his hand to the side of Zalith's neck. "You von't. You know I know vhat I'm doing. You got to see me kill Boreas, avter all," he said confidently. "Vas easy. Zhis vill be no divverent."

Zalith wasn't convinced—well…he didn't *want* to be convinced—but he trusted Alucard. He *had* seen him kill one of the stronger Aegis; it had been something artistic, mesmerizing to watch. Why would it be any different this time? So he tried to focus on *that*. "Okay," he said with a deep exhale.

Alucard took hold of his hand. "Ve'll be okay, I promise," he said with a smile, starting to lead the way again.

The demon smiled again, attempting not only to bury his worry but hide it, too. He didn't want Alucard to think that he had no faith in him. "Do we know much about this drake?" he asked, changing the subject as he walked with his fiancé. "Any sightings?"

"My scouts veported zhat she is maybe a little bigger zhan Drac. She sticks close to zhe cave and only veally leaves to get vood every ozzer day. She 'as been making sure to steer clear of zhe two villages zhat are nearby—vhatever is in zhat cave…zhe Aegis are doing zheir best not to draw attention to or zhemselves."

Zalith nodded. "And what about the dragon that the fur belonged to?"

"Maybe belonged to zhe Aegis zhat vas 'ere bevore Niedreid—uh…Nylrias. Vhenever zhe Aegis are guarding someving, zhey svitch places every vew veeks or so. Mărioara and Gheorghiţă veported zhat Niedreid must 'ave veplaced Nylrias a vew days ago. She is electric dragon—lightning. Very powervul, vone of Levoldus' vight 'ands, I believe. But she 'as moved on to Eastreon."

The demon sighed deeply. His hesitation was getting heavier, and the desire to turn back was almost suffocating him, intensified by every word the vampire said.

"Vhat?" Alucard asked with a frown. "Ve zon't 'ave to deal vith 'er," he repeated. "She moved."

"I hope so," he mumbled.

"Make sure you 'ave your colt veady," the vampire told him, unbuttoning his coat.

Zalith did the same, opening his coat so that he could reach the weapon when he needed it.

"Vhen ve get zhere, ve vill survey zhe area virst and see if Niedreid is in zhe cave. If she is, ve vill lure 'er out—ve vill 'ave a better advantage vighting 'er out 'ere zhan somevhere enclosed. More space to move—ve are quicker zhan 'er. Just vemember: all drakes 'ave zhe ability to disorientate and deaven zheir opponents with a single roar—ve must make our virst priority to take out zhe little vocal cord in 'er neck zhat lets 'er do zhat," he sternly repeated. "I vill use zhe severium I brought to disorientate 'er, and *you* vill vire a vew of zhose vounds into 'er—aim vor zhe parts of 'er body zhat aren't armoured. Zhen, momentarily, *I* vill take out zhe vocal cord and disable 'er ability to disorientate us. Zhen, you can vetreat and I'll vinish 'er off vith Luciverium—you are good vith zhis, no?" he asked, turning his head to look at him.

No. He wanted to say no. He wanted to ask to turn back. But again, he knew that Alucard was capable of this. So, he nodded stiffly. "I'm good."

"Are you sure?" the vampire asked. "You zon't sound so convident."

"I'm confident…I'm just a little worried. Just…my usual need to protect you—it's a little overbearing right now, especially since we're about to fight a giant lizard," he said, trying to attempt a little humour to ease the tension.

Alucard smiled slightly. "I'll be extra carevul, zon't vorry," he said, squeezing Zalith's hand.

"You'd better."

"I vill," he assured him. "Ve are almost zhere," he then mumbled.

Zalith nodded in response.

Without another word, they slipped deeper into the jungle's shadows. The canopy thickened overhead, and the light dimmed, swallowed by layers of mist and leaves. Every step was quieter than the last, every breath a little heavier. Neither of them spoke. The cave lay just ahead, and whatever was inside was waiting.

Chapter Six

— ⸲ † ⸴ —

The Nest

| Alucard |

| *Divinos, Kulogdan, Tigsalanta Territory* |

Alucard kept his gaze fixed ahead, every sense attuned to the shifting jungle around him. Since their arrival in Divinos, he'd been searching for even the faintest trace of an Aegis's aura, but so far, nothing. Not that it surprised him. If Niedreid was anything like Boreas, she was likely using the landscape itself to mask her presence. That kind of manipulation came easily to Aegis, especially in a place this dense with life and ethos. Still, his scouts had sighted her here more than once. She was either off hunting… or watching them from somewhere unseen. Either way, he would find her. And when he did, he would not hesitate.

Cicadas buzzed like a chorus of static in the canopy above. The brush shifted occasionally with the hurried scurry of animals—rabbits, a fox, startled birds—but nothing out of the ordinary yet. No signs of threat. No sudden stillness. But the longer they walked, the harder it became to keep his focus. Zalith was close—too close sometimes. The heat in his blood hadn't lessened; if anything, it was coiling tighter, demanding more. Alucard gritted his teeth. This wasn't the time. Not here. No matter how strong the craving, the mission came first. It had to.

Through the weave of trees ahead, Alucard caught sight of the mountain's base. The rock was a mottled grey-green, streaked with moss and weathered by time, its surface split by deep fractures where small trees clung stubbornly to life. As they neared, the undergrowth gave way, thinning grass turning to packed earth beneath their boots. The trees fell behind them, and they stepped into a wide, barren clearing. The jungle's hum dulled with the shift; even the cicadas, so persistent until now, quieted as if unwilling to cross the invisible threshold.

Alucard slowed their pace, his eyes narrowing as he scanned the terrain. Still no sign of an Aegis' presence. He hadn't sensed a flicker of it since they arrived. Was Niedreid even here? She had to be.

He pressed on, leading them along the mountain's lower reaches, its foothills winding like a fractured spine through the jungle's edge. The cave wasn't far now, just a few more minutes tracing the slope, and if Niedreid wasn't here…he'd use blood magic to search this entire jungle. He wasn't about to waste time.

"What's wrong?" Zalith then asked, snapping him out of his thoughts.

The vampire glanced at him. "I 'aven't been able to locate Niedreid yet," he mumbled. "I've been searching ever since ve arrived. She's probably 'iding 'er aura like Boreas did vhen ve vere in Avalmoor."

A perturbed frown appeared on Zalith's face. "Where would she hide?"

"Vell, zhe cave vor starters. Zhis rock 'as silver veins," he mumbled, tapping the mountain face beside him as he followed it. "'Is 'ard vor me to see vrough. So, if she is inside, I von't be able to tell until ve go in zhere and see vor ourselves. I vould ask you to use your ethos to search vor 'er, but an Aegis can only be detected by anozzer Aegis or somevone vith Numen blood. Some Aegis also 'ave zhe ability to naturally 'ide zheir aura, so…she could be anyvhere."

"We'll keep an eye out," the demon said cautiously.

"I could use blood magic to search zhe entire area," he suggested.

"Is that going to make it hard for you to fight?" Zalith asked.

Alucard shrugged lightly. "I'll be vine—I've vought Aegis in vorse conditions."

Zalith nodded in response.

They walked in silence for a few moments.

And then Zalith said, "I'm sorry if I'm annoying you."

"You're not annoying me," he said with a frown.

"I don't mean to baby you, I'm just worried."

Alucard stopped and shook his head slightly. "You're not. Is okay," he tried to assure him.

Zalith smiled weakly. "Okay."

Although he wasn't sure whether or not his mate had taken his response seriously, Alucard took his hand and continued onwards. They couldn't afford to stand around right now.

"Zhe cave is over zhere," he said, nodding towards the wide, gaping hole in the mountain, accessible from a ledge roughly twenty feet up.

"How do we get in?" Zalith asked as they stopped walking.

"Ve could use my short-distance vhase, but zhere's no guarantee ve'll appear in zhe entrance because of zhe silver. I could vly us up zhere?" he suggested, looking at Zalith.

"Flying works."

The vampire dematerialized them both into vermillion smoke. Almost immediately, they rematerialized at the cave's mouth, where jagged stone framed the entrance like the teeth of a long-dead beast. The air shifted—cooler, damp, and heavy with the scent of old mineral and rot.

A slow exhale echoed faintly from deep within, the kind of sound that didn't belong to wind or beast, but something older, patient, and waiting.

Utter blackness. No flicker of light touched the depths. The walls were slick with condensation, glistening faintly where shafts of dying daylight just barely reached inside. The smell of wet moss clung to the air, threaded through with iron-rich earth, and something else—something acrid and sweet, like breath that had spoiled in the dark.

Even the forest behind them had quieted.

Zalith's grip on Alucard's hand tightened. "Should we go in?" he asked quietly.

The vampire nodded. "She might be in 'ere, so… be prepared vor anyving."

"Okay—just… please be careful."

Focusing on the darkness ahead, Alucard gave a brief nod and murmured, "I vill. Zon't vorry."

He still hadn't detected an Aegis' aura, but the deeper they ventured, the more a strange presence tugged at the edge of his awareness. It wasn't strong enough to be Niedreid, and whatever it was, it didn't feel like an Aegis. Still, it unsettled him. He kept leading them forward, his hand clasped firmly around Zalith's. If something *was* waiting at the end of this tunnel, he'd meet it first, and he'd ensure Zalith never got the chance.

But as the narrow passage opened into a vast, hollowed chamber, Alucard came to a sharp halt.

Zalith stopped at his side.

No Aegis. No enemies. Just silence.

The cavern was massive, its stone walls curving high above them in jagged, uneven rings. The ground was covered in a sprawling bed of grass, branches, and tattered scraps of cloth, fur, and splintered wood. In the centre of it all lay a small, triangular fire pit made of stone and scorched timber. Though the flames had mostly died out, it still smouldered, dark coals pulsing like a heartbeat, casting the cavern in a dim, feverish glow.

And the heat… Alucard could feel it. Unnaturally so. It was definitely of Numen creation. It clung to his skin, like the breath of something too large to see.

His gloved hand twitched at his collar, the instinct to remove his cape growing stronger—but he didn't. He squared his shoulders instead and stepped forward, eyes locked on the fire as its warmth rolled over him in waves. Something had been here recently.

And it might still be close.

Zalith followed closely, his hand slipping free from Alucard's as he stepped slightly ahead, just enough to shield without being obvious. The vampire's gaze flicked to him, watching as his mate unfastened the front of his coat, though not for comfort—he was preparing, readying himself to draw weapons the moment danger surfaced.

As they neared the smouldering fire, the demon moved in beside him again, their bodies brushing together, shoulder to shoulder, hip to hip. Zalith always did that, closed the space between them, quiet and firm, ready to pull him out of harm's way without hesitation.

Alucard didn't speak, but he noticed. He felt it. That silent readiness. That loyalty. And it filled him with a quiet, grounding warmth even as the oppressive heat of the cave clawed at his skin.

He was grateful for it. For *him*.

They stopped in front of the fire, and Alucard stared into it, examining the leaves, the fur, and the flames.

"What is it?" Zalith asked.

Alucard crouched in front of it. "Is…a nest," he realized. "Zhis is vhat zhey vere guarding," he mumbled, looking around.

"Are there any eggs?"

Were there?

The vampire reached into the fire, slow and steady. He felt Zalith flinch beside him, his instincts likely screaming to intervene, but he didn't, and for that, Alucard was quietly grateful.

Carefully, he shifted aside a charred piece of wood, and then he nudged a ring of scorched stones. Heat poured against his skin, but it didn't stop him; it may sting, but it wouldn't injure him. His fingers swept deeper through the embers…and then—

His palm brushed against something.

The surface was blisteringly warm, ridged and uneven like overlapping plates of armour. Not quite scales—thicker than that. Shell-like, but not smooth. Each ridge was dense and faintly grooved, like ancient stone carved by claws. It pulsed faintly with inner warmth, as if something within it slept and breathed.

A slow smile crept across Alucard's lips. Adoration stirred in his chest. "Zhere's an egg," he said, glancing up at his mate.

"Oh, my God," Zalith exhaled like a man mourning peace.

"Vhat?" Alucard scoffed, looking back into the fire.

"You know what."

"I'm not vinking of keeping zhis—is an Aegis ovvspring."

"Sure," Zalith said doubtfully. "You looked at it the way a mother looks at their newborn child for the first time."

Alucard pouted. "Vell…I vhought about vor a moment—b-but…ve can't," he muttered, standing up. "Let's just vind Niedreid and do vhat ve came to do."

Zalith crossed his arms. "Don't worry. I'm sure the egg will hatch, and the baby will imprint on you before we leave."

The vampire scowled. "I zon't vant an Aegis baby."

"Good," Zalith said.

Alucard rolled his eyes and looked around. "Zhere's no sign of 'er in 'ere, so ve'll go outside and I'll use blood magic to search zhe island."

"Okay," the demon said.

The vampire started leading the way back towards the cave entrance. He couldn't help but wonder, however, whether Zalith was mad or not; his snappy 'okay' made it seem as though he was.

"Are you mad?" he asked.

"What?"

"Are you annoyed?" he repeated. "You sound annoyed."

"I'm not annoyed. I'm just worried."

Alucard stared ahead. "I know. But ve're vine. Vhen ve get outside, I'll vind Niedreid; ve can go and kill 'er, and zhen ve'll go 'ome."

"Okay," the demon said, slipping his hand around Alucard's waist and tugging him a little closer as they walked towards the cave's entrance. His voice dropped just enough to make it unmistakably suggestive as he asked, "Can we have sex when we get home?"

Alucard's expression faltered—flustered, caught off guard. He quickly looked away, cheeks tinged with colour as he pouted. "Maybe," he muttered, stubbornly refusing to meet Zalith's eyes.

"You can say no."

"I *vould* say no if I zidn't vant to," he mumbled.

"Your answer wasn't very convincing."

Alucard stopped walking and stared at him, trying to hide his frustration, but it was only becoming worse. "I zon't know." He paused. "Maybe I vill vant to, maybe I von't. I zon't know *vight now*. Ask me again avter ve're done vith zhis dragon," he grumbled, starting to lead the way again.

"Well, now I don't want to."

"Vine."

And then silence.

Alucard kept walking, jaw tight, irritation simmering inside him…though he wasn't even sure who it was aimed at. Was Zalith angry? Upset? Was *he*? The silence between them felt heavier than usual, and Alucard knew he couldn't keep avoiding the conversation he needed to have with the demon.

Zalith was an incubus. Going too long without intimacy wasn't just frustrating, it was physically taxing. And Alucard didn't want to punish him for something that wasn't his fault. He *knew* that. But what else could he do when every time they touched, the weight of inadequacy gnawed deeper?

He didn't feel like a real man. Not when his body reminded him of everything it wasn't. And even though Zalith had never once complained, never once made him feel lesser, the imbalance was still there. Zalith could give so much pleasure with so little effort, and all Alucard could do was take it. It made him feel broken. *Wrong.* Like he was failing in a way he didn't know how to fix.

Maybe it was time to stop putting it off. Maybe Zalith deserved the truth, however ugly it felt.

He halted and grabbed Zalith's wrist, making him stop, too.

"What?" Zalith asked almost tonelessly.

Clearly, he *was* mad. Maybe now wasn't the best time to talk about it.

Alucard let go of his wrist and kept walking. "Never mind," he grumbled.

"What?" Zalith snapped as he followed behind him.

He didn't want to argue. He didn't want to talk about it anymore.

"Hello?" the demon called.

The vampire stopped, exhaled sharply, and turned to face Zalith as he stopped behind him. "Noving," he said irritably. "I'd vather talk about vhen ve get 'ome."

Zalith sighed deeply. "Fi—"

Light—blinding and unnatural—burst through the jungle, searing through Alucard's vision before he could even speak. He saw it reflected in Zalith's eyes, a flicker of something massive and menacing, and then the world detonated.

Pain exploded through him.

He was airborne, slammed backwards by a force so violent that it knocked the breath from his lungs. The impact hit like a freight train, and then the ground rose up to meet him. A dull, cracking *thump* sounded as he struck stone, and then nothing but agony.

Tormenting, all-consuming agony.

He couldn't yell. He couldn't breathe. He couldn't *move.* His limbs were dead weight, molten and crushed, like he'd been dropped into a pool of magma and pinned beneath the surface. Ringing overtook his hearing, white light still dancing behind his eyes.

Where was Zalith?

Had he been hit, too?

The thought pierced through the pain, panic rising in its wake. But Alucard couldn't sit up, he couldn't even lift his head. He could barely think. Every nerve in his body was on fire, and the only thing worse than the pain was the knowledge that something had found them. Something that struck without warning.

And as the earth began to tremble beneath him, soft at first, then harder, deeper, he realized that things were about to get a whole lot worse.

The fight they'd come looking for had found them.

Chapter Seven

— ⸱ ✝ ⸱ —

Storm Bearer

| Zalith |
| *Divinos, Kulogdan, Tigsalanta Territory* |

Zalith lay in a haze of agony, his body a furnace of pain that burned from the inside out. The echo of that blinding strike still rang through his skull, every throb in his head like a hammer blow. His thoughts were fractured, slippery, refusing to piece together. Something had hit them—no, *slammed* into them. Something powerful. And Alucard…Alucard had been right there in front of him when it happened.

Where was Alucard?

Panic gnawed at him, sharper than the pain. He tried to move, he tried to force his body to heal, but nothing responded—not his legs, not his arms. It was as if he were locked inside himself, submerged in molten fire. Every nerve screamed, every breath was a struggle. The torment pressed down like a weight, crushing and drowning, and beneath it all was a single, spiralling thought—if he couldn't move, if he couldn't find Alucard, then maybe…maybe it was already too late.

That light—it felt so familiar…so harrowingly familiar. But how could it be? He struggled, trying to get his body to respond; the ground held him in its grasp, and his panic kept him trapped in torment. What was about to happen?

The ground beneath him shuddered, each deep, earth-shaking thump pounding closer, vibrating through the haze that clouded his mind. Huge, heavy footsteps echoed through the ringing in his skull, feeding the rising dread that clawed at him. He had to move, he had to fight, but his body refused. His limbs lay useless, his senses splintered and blurred. Nothing aligned. Everything was fractured and warped.

Where was he? What was happening? Why was the world nothing but muffled shadows? Why couldn't he *see*? Why couldn't he *hear*? More terrifying still, why couldn't he feel *him*? The life force connection he shared with Alucard was silent, their imprints unresponsive, as if the bond had been cut. His pulse thundered in his chest, racing, panicked, his heart sinking with every beat. There was only one explanation his mind could cling to in that moment, one he couldn't bear to accept.

But slowly and agonizingly, his body began to knit itself back together. The pain still burned through him, but shapes began to sharpen at the edges of his vision, and the piercing ring in his ears ebbed to a dull throb. In its place came a sound far worse.

A guttural snarl.

And Alucard's voice—strained, ragged with pain.

Terror clenched around him like a vice, cutting deeper than any wound. Nothing could drive him harder. He dragged at whatever shreds of strength he could muster, forcing his head to turn, muscles screaming in protest. His arms trembled as he tried to push himself up, the world lurching around him. And through the haze, he saw it. The thing that had struck them down.

A dragon.

Towering close to ten feet, its hide white as fresh snow, arcs of lightning hissed and coiled over its scaled frame like living serpents. Two great wings rose from its back, though one hung twisted and half-shrunken, its membrane puckered and blackened like paper singed in a hearth.

All that mattered was the sight of its massive clawed hand wrapped around Alucard, squeezing and crushing as his blood spilled to the ground.

He wouldn't lie there another heartbeat.

Zalith shoved aside the sting of torn flesh, the warm trickle of his own blood, and the fire of pain clawing through his body. In a single breath, he summoned his demon form; his horns curled from his skull, and his wings tore into being, and he demanded that his ethos respond, giving him the power he needed to reach his fiancé in time.

Then he launched forward, claws unsheathed, fury roaring through every vein. That thing would not keep its grip on his vampire—not for another moment.

The dragon pulled Alucard closer to its face and snarled at him—

Zalith collided with the dragon, striking with all the force his wings could drive, his claws ripping upward in a single, vicious arc. He felt the hot spray of blood across his face as the dragon's grip faltered, its scaled fingers jerking open. Alucard slipped from its grasp and dropped to the ground with a heavy thud, but Zalith had no time to check if he'd risen. His claws had torn *deep*, and with a loud *crack*, the dragon's lower jaw tore free beneath his hands, the weight of it wrenching from sinew and bone.

The creature's scream rattled the cavern, its voice a hollow, guttural wail that shook the stone. Zalith landed between it and his mate, wings flaring wide, muscles thrumming with rage. His chest heaved, his focus narrowing on the beast's lightning-wreathed frame.

Even without her jaw, the dragon staggered upright, a low, throbbing hum building in the mangled remains of her mouth. Lightning danced along her teeth—or what was left of them—congealing into a crackling sphere of white-blue light.

She was going to strike again.

Zalith knew the first blast had nearly broken them both; another would tear them apart. He braced, muscles coiling, ready to hurl himself sideways and drag Alucard with him—

But from the corner of his eye, he saw movement.

Alucard's bloodied hand pressed to the ground, his fingers splayed wide.

The dragon fired.

Zalith moved to dive, but before he could, the floor erupted—shards of glowing luciferium surged upward in a jagged wall between them and the blast. Lightning slammed into the crystalline barrier, refracting outward in a violent storm of sparks that lit the cavern like a tempest.

"Go," Alucard's voice cut through the thunder, firm despite the strain.

Zalith turned his head, his gaze locking with his mate's pale, determined eyes.

"I vill cover you."

The demon did as Alucard said. Despite his overwhelming worry, he burst into action. He let his wings and horns crumble and hurried to the left, leaving the cover of the luciferium barrier. The dragon sharply turned her head, setting her eyes on him as her jaw healed, reforming and reshaping from the gore that remained and streaks of shimmering ethos.

And she didn't waste any time at all in charging another attack. *She fired.*

The lightning came at Zalith so fast that he was sure it was going to hit him, but as his eyes widened, as he prepared to be struck, a huge shard of luciferium broke out from the ground and blocked the lightning, and at the same time, a smaller shard burst up to his left. He knew why; Alucard didn't need to tell him what he had to do. He grabbed the thinner crystal, tore it from the ground, and moved out from behind the luciferium the vampire had created to block the dragon's second attack. And then, before she could defend herself, Zalith launched the shard of luciferium at her.

The dragon's scream split the air as the luciferium shard drove deep into her flank, her lightning flaring in a violent burst. Bolts cracked and snapped outward, searing the air, sparks ricocheting across the cavern like shrapnel. Zalith surged forward, every step shadowed by sudden slivers of luciferium bursting from the ground, intercepting each stray arc that threatened him. He spared a glance towards Alucard, relief cutting through the heat of battle when he saw his vampire was back on his feet.

⇄ **Alucard**

Alucard kept his gaze locked on Zalith, staying low behind the jagged wall of luciferium. Through the shimmer of the crystal, he tracked the demon's movements—swift and relentless, drawing the dragon's attention entirely to himself.

Good. That gave Alucard his opening.

Pain still coiled deep in his bones, harsher now that the creature had crushed him mid-heal, but he forced it aside. The crystals needed to hold; his focus couldn't slip. Ethos bled from him with every second, leaving him weary, but he kept the wall braced, his will dug in like iron.

Then he moved. Leaving the shelter of the luciferium, he sprinted for the dragon, eyes flicking between Zalith and the beast's every twitch. When her body tensed and the crackling glow of another charge built in her maw, Alucard didn't hesitate—he called a shard from the ground, its edges gleaming, and hurled it straight for her face—

Lightning slammed into the stone, missing the egg in the nest's centre by mere inches as Alucard's crystal sliced deep into the dragon's neck. The beast's roar tore through the cavern, a sound of both fury and pain, her massive frame lurching to the side. She snapped her head towards him, eyes blazing, the glow in her throat building for another strike.

But Alucard was already moving. He summoned another shard, heavier this time, and hurled it for Zalith to take. The demon caught it without breaking stride, launching it straight into the dragon's right shoulder. The impact burst with a wet crack; the beast shrieked, her lightning breath veering wide, scorching the air and splintering against the cavern walls. Static leapt and crawled along the stone, sparks dancing like territorial snakes.

Every move and surge of lightning only sharpened Alucard's certainty—this was Nylrias, Storm Bearer, not Niedreid.

And his realization meant he knew exactly what was coming next.

Nylrias reared onto her hind legs, wings spreading wide, one tattered and shrivelled, the other stretching to its full span, and crackling arcs raced across her body until she was shrouded in a storm of her own making.

Alucard cut a glance at Zalith, both still sprinting, both knowing what was about to hit. In a heartbeat, Alucard vanished into a swirl of vermillion smoke, reappearing at the demon's side. His arms locked tight around his mate just as a blinding white light detonated where Nylrias stood.

And then *agony*. That same devouring, searing torment as before, flooding every nerve, crushing every thought, dragging him back into that unrelenting world of pain.

⇄ **Zalith**

Alucard's pained cry tore through Zalith's head, sharper than any wound. The impact of his own back slamming into the stone hardly registered; what he felt was the sudden weight of the vampire sprawled across him. For a heartbeat, his mind reeled, but then clarity snapped into place. Alucard had thrown himself over him—he'd taken the brunt of the blast.

"Alucard," he breathed, forcing himself upright and easing the vampire onto his back.

No response. Just the shallow rise and fall of his chest and a grimace twisted by pain, blood glistening at the corner of his lips.

Rage seared through Zalith's veins, hot enough to burn away the lingering ache in his own body.

If Alucard had been alone, Zalith knew without question that he would have already given himself over to his true form, the form he saved for the direst moments, to rip this dragon apart piece by piece. But Alucard hadn't done that. He hadn't crossed that line, and that meant he still saw another way. And *that* meant he was leaving this fight to Zalith.

Zalith wouldn't fail him.

The choice was made. The dragon would die here.

He pushed to his feet, only then catching sight of the jagged wall of luciferium encircling them—Alucard's doing, no doubt, thrown up in the same instant he'd shoved him clear of the blast. The sight lit a fresh spark of fury in his chest.

With a low breath, he vaulted out from behind the barrier.

The dragon's gaze locked onto him instantly, the air between them humming with the charge she was building. He sprinted straight for her, but instead of gathering power for one devastating strike, she spat lightning in rapid bursts—short, vicious lashes of white-blue heat. Each one cracked the ground where he'd just been, close enough for the ozone to sting his nose.

He slipped between them, ducking and twisting in perfect rhythm, and whenever a bolt came too close, a shard of luciferium flared into being at his flank, splitting the energy harmlessly aside. Alucard was still with him, still fighting through his pain to shield him. But Zalith knew the truth—this kill had to be his.

The demon pressed on, closing the gap as his hand slipped into his coat, fingers curling around the weight of the colt Alucard had given him.

A surge of bright light warned him a heartbeat before the dragon spat a bolt the size of a ballista shot. He dropped low, knees slamming into the stone, and let his speed carry him into a skid. Sparks burst around him as he slid beneath her massive frame, the air sharp with the stench of scorched rock.

He fired one-two-three bullets, each shot driving into the pale scales of her underbelly, the impact thudding through his arms. The dragon's shriek rattled the cavern, and arcs of lightning began to writhe across her body, snapping at the air like whips.

Panic clawed at him—he was too close, too exposed. She lurched sideways and drove one clawed foot down, the stone cracking inches from his head. He rolled away, forcing himself to his feet as another volley of lightning flared.

But something changed. Black, branching veins began to creep over her white scales, an ugly web of death. The light around her flickered and sputtered, and the snarl on her face faltered into something almost fearful.

Without thought, Zalith surged forward. The memory of Alucard bringing down Boreas flashed in his mind—he kicked off the ground, adorning his wings and horns, and shot into the air; a shard of luciferium cut past his left side, and his hand snapped out, catching it. With a beat of his wings, he twisted, driving himself down in a sharp arc, and hurled the crystal straight for the dragon's skull just as she lunged upward, jaws gaping for him.

She screamed as the shard in his hand punched deep into her shoulder. Lightning flared in a chaotic burst around her—but then a much larger spear of luciferium ripped past him from Alucard's direction, slamming into her chest with bone-cracking force.

Zalith swept through the chaos, wings slicing the air as he darted over and between the ragged beats of her tattered wings. Another shard came spinning towards him, and he caught it without slowing; he pivoted mid-flight and hurled it down with all his strength. It struck square between her wings, driving deep enough to hammer her down onto the stone floor.

The dragon roared, claws gouging trenches into the ground as she tried to push herself up. But Alucard was already moving. One last shard streaked through the air, biting into the side of her neck.

Zalith's eyes snapped to him—Alucard's right hand rose. A pulse of power rippled through the cavern, and in the next breath, every shard buried in the dragon detonated at once.

The explosion ripped her apart from within—muscle, blood, and fragments of white scale showered the cavern alongside a storm of red-black luciferium shards, the air thick with heat and the stench of scorched flesh.

It was over.

Zalith landed a few feet from the mangled body of what was once Nylrias; she was still breathing, gurgling as blood spilled from so many gaping holes in her body.

He hurried to Alucard, who stood there, barely able to keep himself on his feet. The demon grabbed him, wrapping his arms around him as he stumbled forward. "Alucard...."

The vampire shook his head. "Is not vinished," he said, moving Zalith away.

He stepped aside, trying to fight the urge to pull him back into a tight embrace. But he remembered that when Alucard killed Boreas, he'd done something after…he'd completely eradicated Boreas' body. He assumed he wanted to do the same here—but…didn't he want the dragon's fur?

Alucard lifted his left hand, fingers curling as if closing around something unseen. A faint black glow bloomed in his palm, and in that instant, what was left of the dragon's eyes darkened to bottomless voids, and her convulsing, blood-slick body went slack.

Zalith watched as the change swept through her. Flesh blanched, flaking into white dust that drifted from bone, pulled inexorably towards the glow in Alucard's hand. Even the scorched hide dissolved until only a great, bleached skeleton and a ragged pelt of fur clung stubbornly to her frame.

In the span of heartbeats, the last of her essence condensed—a small, luminous crystal of deep violet coalesced in Alucard's palm, shimmering once before collapsing inward, its light swallowed by a black hexagonal talisman etched with faintly glowing runes.

It began to fall, but Alucard snatched it before it could hit the stone. The triumph lasted only a breath, though. His knees buckled, and the talisman slipped from his grasp—

Zalith lunged, catching him before he struck the ground. He lowered with him, cradling him close, wings folding protectively around them both.

The cavern was silent.

Now it was over.

Zalith looked down at him, distress tightening in his chest. He shifted one hand to the side of Alucard's face, his thumb brushing lightly against cool skin. "Are you okay?" he asked softly.

Alucard's eyes closed, the rigid tension in his body easing as he gave a small, wordless nod in the demon's hold.

Zalith's fingers slid into his hair, cradling him closer. The thought of how close he'd come to losing him threatened to hollow him out. What would he have done if that dragon had taken Alucard from him? The question clawed at him, unwanted, unanswerable. He forced it back, scowling faintly at the weight in his chest.

The dragon was dead. It was over. All that mattered now was keeping his vampire safe and making sure he recovered.

"Do you want blood?" he asked, staring down at him.

Alucard didn't immediately answer. He lay there, his erratic breathing slowly calming.

Zalith waited, letting him rest while he caressed his hair, holding him. But the longer he waited, the more worried he began to feel. "Alucard?"

The vampire responded with a quiet murmur of acknowledgement.

"You need blood," he insisted, rolling up his sleeve. "Please."

Alucard exhaled deeply as he slowly opened his eyes. "She vasn't meant to be 'ere. Vas…meant to be a drake."

"I know, baby. It's okay."

He shook his head. "No," he mumbled with a distraught frown. "Is my vault—I should 'ave been paying attention."

With his concern growing, Zalith shook his head and moved his exposed wrist closer to Alucard's mouth. "It's not your fault," he told him. "We couldn't detect the dragon. What matters is that you're okay—that's all I really care about. Now please," he pleaded gently. "Alucard, you need to heal."

Alucard frowned hesitantly. He looked like he was checking him over for wounds first.

"I'm okay, I promise," he assured him.

The vampire still searched, but then he lightly gripped Zalith's wrist and pulled it closer to his mouth.

When Alucard's fangs pierced his skin and sank into him, a hushed groan left Zalith, the euphoria of his venom quickly enthralling him. He stifled a pleased moan as he watched his fiancé swallow his blood, gulping quietly but eagerly. It shoved aside his worry and dismay, urging his desires to resurface; he did his best to fight it all, though. He needed to remain focused.

Alucard then released his arm. "Vank you," he sighed, closing his eyes, his pale face smothered with relief and delight.

Zalith nodded, caressing his mate's hair again. The dismay hadn't faded much; all he wanted to do was sit there and hold his vampire. Seeing him so hurt broke his heart. It filled him with despair, and his throat was so tight and his body so stiff. He never wanted to have to go through anything like that ever again.

"Ve can…vest 'ere vor a bit," Alucard mumbled, moving his hand up and over Zalith's chest to grip his shoulder. "Maybe just…ten minutes."

"Are we safe?" he asked. "Is anyone going to notice that she's dead?"

He shook his head. "I 'id 'er ethos, so no vone vill know unless zhey see 'er body, and zhat von't 'appen until is time vor zhe next Aegis to take 'er place."

The demon nodded again. He was too distressed to say much. But they both needed to rest—only for a moment, though. The sooner they left this place, the better.

While they sat there, Zalith felt his mind begin to drift. A heaviness settled in his chest—not just exhaustion, but the quiet, gnawing truth that he was tired of all this. The endless fighting. The pain. The constant risk that one day Alucard wouldn't get back up. What he wouldn't give to keep him safe, to see him live without a single scar more.

He had thought he was ready for this war, but the truth was beginning to sink in. It was going to be far harder than he'd imagined. This hadn't even been a Numen, and still they'd come within a breath of death. If they could barely survive an Aegis, how were they supposed to stand against Lilith and Damien?

He didn't really care about his own safety. All that mattered was Alucard—and the gut-twisting, mortifying fear of what would happen if he lost him.

Something had crossed his mind back in Atheson not long ago. If he and Alucard were mate-bonded, they'd heal faster when skin-to-skin. Maybe he should bring it up—no, he *would* bring it up. But not now. Now, he just wanted to hold his vampire.

He couldn't start doubting himself, either. He had an army ready for when the time came to face the Numen. Not only had they been alone this time, but they'd also not been prepared for this lightning-wielding dragon; they'd come ready for a drake.

Zalith didn't want to think too much about it. Alucard was okay, and the battle was over. They'd got what they had come for…and now it was time to head home.

Chapter Eight

— ≷ ✝ ≷ —

The Baby

| Alucard |
| *Divinos, Kulogdan, Tigsalanta Territory* |

Alucard exhaled deeply, relaxing in Zalith's arms, but he shouldn't get comfortable. They couldn't stay there much longer.

He'd send Nylrias' fur to where he stored his valuables, and once he had recovered, he'd get to work on crafting with it. For now, though, he wanted to focus on getting home. Zalith had also been hit by the Aegis' strikes, and he wanted to make sure *he* was okay.

"Alucard?" Zalith asked quietly, fiddling with his hair. "I think it's time for us to leave. Can you walk?"

The vampire frowned, opening his eyes to stare up at him. His body felt better; he wasn't in so much agony anymore. Zalith's blood had helped with that. So he nodded in response, and as the demon helped him to his feet, he exhaled deeply. They couldn't leave just yet, though.

He looked over at Nylrias' skeleton and scowled. "I 'ave to take zhe vur."

"It's okay," Zalith said. "Let me do it."

Alucard frowned. "You vill…sit zhere and skin dragon?" he asked, smirking as best he could, trying to hide the fact that standing had aggravated his healing wounds.

"No…but I can put it somewhere safe so a professional can sit at his worktable and skin it for you—"

"*I* am zhe provessional…and if ve send zhat to somevone else, zhe guy vill probably vun off vith and sell to people ve zon't vant getting 'old of someving so precious," he insisted, making his way over to the skeleton. "And I zon't trust anyvone else. I vill send to vhere I keep all my ozzer vings, and zhen I vill vork on during zhe veek."

"Okay," Zalith laughed. "I didn't know that you did all of that yourself—don't worry; I won't send it off to someone."

Without further discussion, Alucard prepared to store the bones—

But Zalith lightly grabbed his wrist and pulled him back. "I can put it away. I want you to relax."

"I'm vine," he tried to assure him. "Vill only take a vew minutes."

"No," his mate denied.

Alucard pouted. "Vhat are you going to cut vith, 'uh?" he tested.

"Alucard," Zalith said amusedly, standing beside the dragon's skeleton, "I'm just putting it away for you so you can do whatever you need to do to it when we get back. Calm down."

Glaring at him, Alucard crossed his arms and pouted stubbornly. "Vine," he grumbled.

As Zalith started transporting the dragon using his ethos, Alucard sighed and observed. Now that it was over, he couldn't help but wonder… why was Nylrias here instead of Niedreid? His scouts had reported seeing Nylrias leave and Niedreid take her place.

It didn't really matter anymore. Nylrias was dead, and all Alucard wanted to do was get home and move on.

Once Zalith finished sending the Aegis' remains to the vault in their castle, Alucard prepared to fly them both home.

Something rustled behind them.

Alucard looked over his shoulder. The sound came again; this time, he pinpointed where it was coming from. He left Zalith's side and headed over to the azul fire in the centre of the cavern.

Something was moving around inside.

Was the egg hatching?

He slowly reached into the flames, his hand meeting the ridge-covered shell.

"I thought you didn't want an Aegis," Zalith suddenly muttered, appearing behind him.

A little startled, Alucard pulled his hand from the fire and grumbled, "I zon't."

The demon laughed softly. "Then leave it alone."

Alucard looked up at him. "I vink is 'atching."

"Just in time for you to take it home."

Looking back into the fire, he shook his head. "Ve can't… vell… I zon't know," he mumbled. But as the egg rattled and cracked, he stood up and stepped back.

The flames guarding the egg flickered and thinned, their glow retreating until only embers clung to the air. With a final tremor, the egg tipped free of the fire, rolling onto the nest of fur and splintered wood built carefully around it. Alucard stood beside Zalith, unsure whether to move or simply watch. The shell quivered and splintered, sharp cracks racing across its surface. Whatever lay inside was fighting to break free…and it seemed desperate to meet the world.

With a conflicted frown, he looked at Zalith. "Vhat do ve do?"

"Is it hard to raise a dragon?" he asked as the egg continued rattling, and a small crack crept up its left side.

Alucard shrugged. "I've only ever vaised Drac, and 'e's not an Aegis."

"Is it possible that the baby can be tracked by the Numen?"

"Yes…unless ve made so zhey can't," he mumbled.

"How?"

"Vhy does matter? Ve can't keep zhe ving," he mumbled, looking down at the egg as the top started cracking.

Zalith shrugged. "Okay. Let's go," he said, turning around.

"Vhat?" Alucard questioned confusedly, looking back at him. "Ve can't just…leave 'im 'ere—'e vill die," he said, his gaze returning to the egg as small pieces of its shell broke off, revealing white scales inside.

"So what do we do, then?" Zalith asked, making his way back over to him.

He shrugged, glancing around the cavern. "Vell…ve could…I zon't know…maybe ve could…take 'im?" He pouted, staring down at the egg again.

"And *not* keep it?"

He shrugged again. "Vell…I guess ve could…drop 'im off somevhere or someving," he mumbled—but in reality, he did actually want to keep this baby dragon.

"Like where?"

"I zon't know—maybe vhere anozzer Aegis is."

"So, if that's the plan, shouldn't we just leave it here and hope the dragon we were actually looking for will take care of it?"

"Ve 'ave no idea vhere she is. In zhe time takes 'er to get 'ere, anyving could come into zhis cave and eat 'im," he said, nodding down at the egg—

A scaled foot suddenly burst through the top of the egg, shards of shell scattering like splintered porcelain.

Both of them instinctively stepped back, watching as the white, scale-clad limb wriggled frantically. The egg tipped onto its side, the leg kicking against the ground in sharp, erratic bursts, sending the shell spinning across the nest.

"Aren't things supposed to hatch face-first?" Zalith asked.

Staring at the spinning egg, Alucard nodded. "Zhey are."

An abrupt crack split the air as a wing punched through the other side of the egg, the small limb stamping against the ground to halt the spinning shell. The two of them watched as the egg shuddered, fractured, and finally collapsed in on itself.

From the wreckage tumbled a creature no larger than a cat, landing clumsily on its front with its back to them. It gave a faint, plaintive squeak. Its scaled body was a pale, ashen white, a soft silver mane encircling its head and trailing down its spined neck to the tip of its tail, where a jagged spike gleamed faintly in the firelight. Four stubby horns jutted from the crown of its head, and as it wobbled upright on awkward hind legs and half-formed wings, it shook itself like a wet dog, sending shell fragments skittering across the ground.

Then, without warning, it spun around to face them—wide, bright blue eyes staring up at them... all six of them. Alucard blinked. Six. And somehow, impossibly, that only made it more endearing. His chest gave a small, involuntary ache of fondness, and he had to stop himself from scooping it up on the spot.

The hatchling tilted its head from side to side, gaze flicking between Zalith and him as though weighing its options. Zalith. Alucard. Zalith again. Alucard decided he wasn't about to wait for its verdict. He stepped forward, hands half outstretched—

But the little dragonlet sprang into motion, darting straight for Zalith. Before Alucard could react, it was clawing and scrabbling up the demon's leg. Zalith stepped back, staring at him with a look that hovered somewhere between helplessness and mild disgust.

Alucard closed the gap in two strides, reaching to lift the creature away—but it hissed sharply in his face and darted behind Zalith's legs, using the demon as a living barricade.

"What is it doing?" Zalith asked, staring down at it and trying to move away, but every time he took a step, the dragon followed, clinging to his leg.

Stepping back, convinced that he wasn't going to be able to grab the dragon, Alucard frowned, crossed his arms, and pouted. "Obviously, she 'as chosen *you* to look avter 'er," he grumbled.

"Why?"

"I zon't know," he sneered. "Probably because she saw you virst—dragons imprint on zhe virst ving zhey see. Looks like you are 'er Mommy now, Zaliv," he said with a smirk, watching as the dragon tried to climb up Zalith's leg again but kept sinking back down to the ground.

She then pounced up higher than before and sank her wing-talons into Zalith's trousers... and that was where she hung, clinging to his leg behind his knee, swaying her tail from side to side as she gazed up at him.

The revolted expression hadn't left Zalith's face. "What am I supposed to do?"

"Pick 'er up."

The demon didn't look *at all* happy. "Really?" he asked, deadpan.

"If I vere you, I'd do bevore she starts crying," he said, nodding down at the dragon as she tried to climb higher up Zalith's leg.

"What if she bites me?"

"I zon't vink she vill—and even if she did, she von't 'ave any teeth yet."

With a very uncomfortable frown, Zalith reached down and pried the dragon from his leg. He lifted her and held her out in front of himself as if she were some sort of disgusting rodent. "Can you take it?" he asked Alucard.

Clearly, his mate wanted nothing to do with it. So he held out his hands—but when Zalith was about to hand her over, the dragon wriggled around and broke free before Alucard could grab her. She scurried across the ground again and latched herself onto Zalith's shin, glaring up at Alucard like he was a monster.

Irritated, trying to hide the fact that he was actually jealous that this dragon had chosen Zalith as her mother over him, he crossed his arms and scoffed. "She zoesn't like me. *You* 'ave to take 'er."

"I'm sure she likes you, she's just shy," Zalith argued, picking her up again, trying to hand her to him—

Distressed chirps came from the dragon as she leapt out of the demon's hands and latched onto his chest, spreading her wings so that she could grip his shoulders.

Alucard scowled and impatiently tapped his foot on the ground. "Veally?" he grumbled. "Because looks like she vinks you're 'er Mom, Zaliv."

"But I'm not her Mom," he said, moving closer to Alucard. He leaned over, clearly hoping that the dragon would leave him and latch onto the vampire—

"She vinks you are, so you are," Alucard said simply, walking away and heading to the cave entrance. As much as he wanted the dragon to think that *he* was its mother, he knew that there would be no changing her mind. She'd imprinted on Zalith, and that was that. "Let's go," he called.

Zalith hurried to catch up with him and walked at his side. "Why are you grouchy?" he asked, walking with the dragon still sprawled across his chest. "I'd prefer things the other way around."

"Vell, zhey're not. She chose you, so you 'ave to take care of 'er."

"I...don't know how," the demon said, sounding worried.

Alucard shrugged. "Zhere are plenty of books in zhe library."

The demon sighed deeply.

"Or...I could teach you," he mumbled.

"Maybe," Zalith replied.

Alucard set his eyes on him. "Are you actually going to take care of 'er? You 'ave to name 'er, too."

"I thought we were taking her to one of the other Aegis."

"Vell...she imprinted on you. She von't take to anozzer dragon now. If ve do zhat, she vill starve and die," he said sadly.

With a conflicted gaze, Zalith's eyes landed on the dragon once more. But as each moment stretched on, he looked more and more unsure.

"You're not going to get vid of 'er...are you?" Alucard asked sullenly.

Zalith looked at him. "No," he said, but his tone was indiscernible.

"Good," the vampire said firmly, staring ahead as they approached the cave entrance. "You 'ave to name 'er, zhough," he repeated.

He shook his head. "I want you to name her."

"No. She's your baby. *You* 'ave to."

"You're the one who wanted her in the first place—and she's *our* baby."

"Vell, you're zhe vone she imprinted on."

"That's fine. You can still pick her name."

"I zon't vant to," he grumbled.

"You don't want to name our baby?"

"I can't name 'er," Alucard insisted as they stepped out of the cave and into the light of day once more. "Aegis are like zemons; zhe parent zhey imprint on 'as to name zhem."

"Okay, so…you pick the name and then I'll give her the name."

Alucard sighed and glared down at the ground. "I zon't know. Ve can vink of someving vhen ve get 'ome."

The demon nodded. "Okay."

Chapter Nine

— ⸢ † ⸣ —

Feeding Time

| **Alucard** |
| *Aestrael, Uzlia Isles, Usrul, Castle Reiner* |

Rain battered the castle windows, each flash of lightning throwing the kitchen into a brief, white glare before the shadows swallowed it again. Thunder rolled overhead, low and constant, like a warning that refused to fade.

The little dragon was still hooked to Zalith's coat, claws dug in stubbornly as she craned her neck to stare up at him with those big, ridiculous eyes. Alucard followed a few steps behind, watching her adoration with something sharp and sour in his chest. She hadn't spared him a glance the whole way back.

Fine. Let her cling to Zalith. What mattered was keeping her alive and making sure she got what she needed, whether she'd chosen the right person or not. Zalith didn't know the first thing about dragons, and if she was going to rely on him, then Alucard would have to help make sure that she didn't starve or wither.

Still…Zalith was listening; he was actually paying attention as Alucard told him what to prepare for. That counted for something…even if every flash of lightning lit up the sight of her pressed close to him, as if she'd never let go.

"What does it eat?" was Zalith's next question.

"Dragonlets eat vhatever zheir mothers can vind—usually vish and small mammals. Zheir parents also vegurgitate zhe vood into zhe baby's mouth…like birds."

The demon's face contorted into a revolted frown. "Ew," he groaned. "How long do we have to feed her for?"

"Until 'er teeth start coming vhrough."

"Do you know how long until that happens?"

Alucard shrugged. "A vew veeks, maybe."

His mate nodded.

"Uh…c-can I help you, sirs?" one of the chefs asked as he emerged from the storage room with a saucepan and some sort of cooking…utensil…thing, its name a mystery to Alucard.

"You can," the vampire replied. "I vant you to prepare some vish and zhen…mash up," he instructed.

"Mash…it?" the man asked unsurely, raising an eyebrow.

"Yes, zhat's vhat I said. Is vor baby."

The chef nodded, but his eyes drifted from Alucard to Zalith—and when he obviously noticed the dragonlet clinging onto Zalith's shoulders, the man gasped, *"Oh, my dearest God. What in the world?! Oh, my. Oh, my, my, my, another creature—what is so wrong with normal pets?!"* in Lupanese as he hurried off to do as he'd been told.

Alucard rolled his eyes at the man, and then he turned to Zalith. "Ve can take 'er to zhe sheltered garden," he suggested.

Zalith nodded. "Okay. Lead the way."

"'Ave you vhought of a name yet?" the vampire asked, heading towards one of the patio doors.

"Have *you*?"

He half shrugged. "No."

"Then no, I haven't."

They stepped out into the sheltered garden, the soft patter of rain on the glass roof above mixing with the heavier drumming of the storm beyond. The walls were open to the air, but thick hedges and climbing roses softened the wind's bite. Grass stretched underfoot, damp with the cool spray drifting in, and beyond it bloomed a scatter of night-scented flowers—violets, lilies, daisies, and pale moon-blooms glowing faintly in the stormlight. A pair of young fruit trees, their leaves trembling, arched over one side of the space, heavy with rain-speckled blossoms.

Another flash of lightning lit the garden in stark white. Alucard's gaze caught on the dragonlet still clinging to Zalith, her six eyes wide, all fixed upward. She didn't even flinch at the thunder that followed. No, she was *transfixed*. Alucard was certain he knew why: the Aegis that had guarded her, likely her mother, possessed lightning ethos.

His chest ached with something he didn't want to name. Pouting, he mumbled softly, almost sadly, "I vant *you* to name 'er."

"I want *you* to name her," Zalith replied.

"I vant *you* to name 'er—she's your baby," Alucard argued.

"Well, *you're* my baby too, and that's why I want you to name her."

Alucard couldn't help but smile a little. But he quickly pouted, sighed, and gave in. They'd be arguing about it all day if he didn't. "Vell…" he mumbled, thinking as they crossed the grass through the garden. "I knew somevone vonce—zhey vere called

Morgana. I veally like zhat name, so…maybe Morgana? Or, if you vant someving simple, ve can just call 'er Shelly," he said with an amused smirk.

"We're *not* calling her Shelly," Zalith denied. "I'll have to think about Morgana, though."

"I can vink of ozzer vings…if you vant," he said, stopping beside one of the benches.

The demon nodded. "I'd like that. Thank you."

They sat, and at last the dragonlet loosened her hold, slipping from where she'd been draped like a living necklace around Zalith's neck. She shifted down into his lap, a coil of ashen scales and silver mane. Another flash of lightning lit the garden, its reflection sparking in all six of her eyes; she tilted her head to the sky, mesmerized for a heartbeat, before settling again, curling tightly into herself. And there she stayed.

"She veally likes you," Alucard said, smiling down at the small dragon.

"I don't know why," Zalith mumbled, relaxing.

He shrugged and smirked as he said, "Vell, you've been talking about 'aving a baby. Now you 'ave vone."

"Not really what I meant, but…I guess you're right."

With a content hum, Alucard rested his head on his mate's shoulder—

The dragonlet immediately lifted her head and hissed at him.

He frowned, scowled, and took his eyes off her, ignoring her as she snarled quietly.

With a soft sigh, Zalith rested his head on Alucard's.

Silence wrapped around them, not as a constricting serpent but as a calming warmth. It was peaceful. It was safe.

But—

But….

*Of course…*Alucard sank into his thoughts. He *always* did when the silence stretched on a moment too long.

Before Nylrias attacked them, he and Zalith hadn't exactly had the best of conversations. He was convinced that he'd either upset his mate or made him angry— maybe even both. And he felt guilty.

"I'm sorry vor making you mad earlier," he murmured disappointedly. He felt ashamed of himself. Zalith hadn't done anything wrong—Zalith didn't even know what it was all about.

"It's okay," Zalith said gently. "I wasn't mad."

"I'm still sorry."

"Don't worry about it, baby."

Alucard exhaled through his nose and closed his eyes. "I vas awvul to you—I snapped, and…I zidn't mean to. I'm just…tired, and I still vind 'ard to control myselv sometimes. I'm sorry," he repeated, moving his head to nuzzle the demon's neck. That was part of it, yes, but so were the frustration and feelings of inferiority. He should tell him, but…he felt so…so…was there even a word for it? Revolting? Strange. Abnormal. Zalith told him that the fact that he wasn't a real man didn't bother him, but he couldn't accept that…no matter how many times in his head he replayed the moment Zalith assured him of it.

And not to mention the heat. It was still there…simmering beneath the overbearing emotions currently devouring him.

"It's okay." Zalith moved his arm around him. "I forgive you." But he sounded upset.

As the shame and guilt grew, Alucard leaned into Zalith a little more. "If you're upset vith me, is okay. You can be mad at me."

The demon shook his head. "I'm not mad, I promise. I'm just…sad."

That was worse than mad. "I'm veally sorry," he lamented.

"Not because of you," he told him quickly, caressing his hair. "I—" He cut himself off with a sharp huff. "All that bright light made me think that Adellum was back. I thought I was going to lose you, Alucard." His embrace tightened around him. "And I just need to be close to you right now." A pause…long…tense…as if he were considering his next words carefully. "I love you," were those words. "More than I've ever loved anything. I can't bear the thought of a life without you."

Alucard shook his head, nuzzling the side of Zalith's face as his hand pressed against his neck. "I'm never going anyvhere, my love. Ve belong to each ozzer vorever, and noving vill change zhat."

Another quiet breath left Zalith—he did that when he was trying to fight back his emotions…and he clearly won the battle. He kissed Alucard's head and quietly breathed in his scent. "You're right," he murmured.

He wouldn't push him to tell him what was going on inside his head; Alucard already had a pretty good idea, and he knew that his mate would appreciate him leaving it alone. So he did.

As he rested his head on the demon's shoulder, he glanced down at the dragonlet, who was still glaring up at him, looking like she was going to pounce any moment. But then she looked to her right, and Alucard followed her gaze.

Edwin was standing not far from the door with a bowl in his hands…and a wary look on his face. "As requested, sirs," he said humbly.

Alucard looked at Zalith and curiously asked, "Are you going to veed 'er?"

"Hmm?" the demon replied before he turned his head, and when he noticed Edwin, he shrugged. "I guess…unless she'll let you do it."

Alucard shook his head as he got up and took the bowl and a syringe from Edwin. "*You* 'ave to do," he insisted, sitting back down. He dipped the syringe into the soupy fish mixture, and once he filled it, he held it out to Zalith. "Veed your baby," he teased him.

Zalith gave a long-suffering sigh. "Okay," he murmured, taking the syringe with the air of a man who'd just been handed a fatally venomous snake.

Alucard's smile deepened as he watched him—how the demon's hand moved tentatively over the dragonlet's back, his other hand holding the syringe just so, as though afraid to scare her off. The little creature's head lifted, nostrils flaring at the scent of fish, eyes fixing sharply on the offering. Zalith brought the syringe closer, and she sat up, tilting her head with a curious chirp. For a moment, she seemed to deliberate, gaze darting between the syringe and the demon's face, as if weighing her trust. Then, surprisingly, she leaned forward and latched her toothless mouth over the tip, gulping eagerly.

"She must be so 'ungry," Alucard said, putting the bowl down beside him as he watched Zalith feed the baby dragon.

"She must be," Zalith agreed. "She's had a long day—we all have."

The vampire rested his head on Zalith's shoulder again, and just as she had before, the dragonlet hissed protectively, pushing aside the food-filled syringe with her face so that she could glare at Alucard.

"Maybe ve should 'ave an early night, no?" the vampire suggested, glancing down at her.

"Maybe," the demon mumbled. "Do you know how often I need to feed her?" he asked as she ate from the syringe again, keeping a close, skeptical eye on Alucard.

"Hmm… vrom vhat I know… six times a day."

"Six?"

"At least," Alucard confirmed.

Zalith sighed. "Okay. If you could direct me to the dragon books in the library, that would be helpful."

"I can bring vone vor you to vead in bed tonight," he said with a smile.

Zalith finished feeding the dragonlet. "Thank you," he replied.

He nodded. "Vhat do you vant to do vith zhe vest of our day?"

The demon put the empty syringe down and let the dragonlet curl up in his lap. "Work, I guess," he said, relaxing once again. "If you're feeling up to it, maybe you should start working on the dragon fur."

Alucard didn't really feel like working. "Ve should both vest," he suggested quietly. "You vere veally 'urt earlier—you should velax," he said, moving his hand over Zalith's chest. "I could vead to you," he suggested.

A smile flickered across Zalith's face as he said, "I would like that." Then came the worried frown. "I'm worried someone might find out that we were in Divinos, though, so I'm going to send some people over there to cover our tracks. I also need to get this dragon hidden; I won't be comfortable resting until I get that done."

As much as he wanted to try and get Zalith to relax, he knew that he was right. "Do you need my 'elp vith anyving?"

"No, it's okay. You can relax."

He frowned sullenly. "Can I come and keep you company vhile you vork?"

"Yeah, if you'd like."

"Vhat vill you do vith 'er vhile you vork?" he asked, looking down at the dragonlet.

"That's another thing I have to figure out. She's going to need somewhere to sleep, and based on how clingy she seems to be already, she's going to need somewhere to sit in my office and the main areas of the house. She's fine for now, but when she gets bigger, it's going to get annoying."

Alucard shrugged. "Dragons lose zheir clinginess zhe older zhey get—Drac did, anyvay. You'll be vree of 'er soon enough."

"I don't know…Drac seems pretty clingy."

"I miss Drac," he mumbled, pouting.

"Maybe we can visit him sometime soon," the demon suggested.

"I zon't know," he said, slouching back. "'E seems 'appy vith 'is girlvriend—maybe 'e vorgot about me."

"How could anyone forget about you?" Zalith asked sadly, tucking a few strands of his hair behind his ear.

He shrugged. "I zon't know," he spoke almost indistinctively.

"He'll be very happy to see you, baby. Don't worry."

Sabazios suddenly barked and came running over—

The moment she heard him, the dragonlet lifted her head, set her eyes on the approaching hellhound—who was soaking wet from the rain—and arched her body up to make herself look bigger, a lot like a cat. And then she hissed.

Sabazios stopped in his tracks and glared at her, tilting his head and flicking his ears as rainwater cascaded from his thick coat like several tiny waterfalls.

Seconds later, Zalith pointed at the hound and then to the far end of the sheltered area. "Go," he said firmly. "You're not allowed inside until you've dried off."

The hound whined quietly but turned around and slowly dragged himself to where he'd been told.

"I vink 'e vants to be ved, too," Alucard said and stood up. "Should I meet you in your ovvice vhen I'm done?"

"Okay," the demon said. He gently grasped the vampire's wrist and pulled him closer, making him lean down, and then he kissed his lips.

Alucard smiled again. "I love you," he said quietly. "I shouldn't be too long." And then he turned around and headed inside.

Chapter Ten

— ⸱ † ⸱ —

A Little Bite

| **Zalith** |

| *Uzlia Isles, Usrul, Castle Reiner* |

Lightning flashed through the windows, lighting Zalith's office every once in a while.

And with every burst, his heart raced a little faster. He knew that it was just lightning; he knew it was only the storm outside. But the part of him scarred by Adellum insisted that it was *him*, that he was coming to take Alucard from him.

He exhaled deeply and tried focusing on his work. Spread in a loose fan across his desk were papers and reports. There was more than enough for him to bury himself in: the Detainer situation—the team he'd assigned to follow the Mirewharf survivor had sent their first report, but there were no answers yet. Tyrus, Orin, Crowell, and Nymeris hadn't found Lucious yet, either, but they had a lead. And the sculptor he'd commissioned had sent sketches of the monument he and Alucard had talked about.

Beneath the window to his left, the small bed that Alucard had set out for the dragonlet sat untouched—at least for long. She had abandoned it minutes ago, scurrying across the floor and hauling herself into his lap as if she belonged there. Now she was curled against him, warm and faintly rumbling, but Zalith kept his attention fixed on the work in front of him. He didn't have the time—or the luxury—to fuss over her right now.

On the bookshelf to the right, an izuret waited patiently, its huge yellow eyes gawping at him. The way those creatures stared might unsettle anyone else, but he was used to it—he was used to *them* and their odd behaviour. He'd not change anything about them, though.

Once he finished reading and closed one of the files, he turned to face the creature—Rook was his name, chosen when he first laid eyes on a rook chess piece, the very piece he wore around his neck on a black metal chain.

"I need you to go and find Silvannus. He's stationed just outside of Atheson City. Tell him to take a few of his covenant and make sure that nobody knows Alucard and I were in Divinos today. He'll know what to do."

Rook saluted.

Zalith paid the creature; as usual, Rook took a chess piece; he probably had enough to complete a few sets by now. And then he vanished in a puff of yellow smoke.

With a quiet exhale, he leaned back in his seat. There was still more to do. He had to hide the dragonlet, which he'd been thinking about. Maybe he could get collars for *all* the animals and have them enchanted just like his own chain and the ring he'd given Alucard. The sooner the dragonlet was hidden, the better. Of course, Uzlia was surrounded by countless protective wards and the Aestrael Curve, but he just wanted to be extra safe.

But covering up their visit to Divinos wasn't the only thing pressing on him. The day's events still gnawed at the edges of his mind. It had been far too easy for Nylrias to ambush them; it had been far too easy for that Aegis to bring them both down. Yes, they'd been distracted, but distraction was no excuse. Next time, there would be no weakness, no blind spot left for an enemy to exploit. He would see to it that they were prepared for every possible turn because the sight of Alucard bleeding, broken, and struggling to stand…that image had carved itself into him.

And he would not see it repeated.

"Are you vinished?" came Alucard's voice

Zalith looked up from his work and gazed across the room at him. Seeing him lying there comfortably on the couch was a relieving sight. It calmed him a little, enough to regain some of his focus. "Not yet," he told him, resting his arms on his desk. "I do need to talk to you about something, though."

Alucard frowned as worry flickered across his pale face. "Vhat?"

"I was thinking about it…and we should get protective collars for Peaches and Sabazios…and the dragonlet, too—just in case. They're easily recognizable. But…we'd have to get Magnus involved."

The vampire sat up, placing his book down beside him. "I zon't like Opus," he grumbled, hostility sharpening both his voice and his frown. He slouched back in his seat. "Can't ve vind somevone else?"

"I don't like him either, but who else out there can do it?"

Alucard crossed his arms with a shrug. "You said you knew a vizard long time ago, vone who could 'ide me vrom Zamien. Vhat about 'im?"

Zalith shrugged, too. "I think it's safe to assume that anyone who didn't come over from Eltaria with us is dead."

The vampire sighed with a displeased glare. "And ve zon't veally 'ave zhe time or vesources to look vor somevone else, do ve?"

"Not really," he answered.

"Zhis is zhe kind of shit zhat makes me vish I'd been taught 'ow to use my vitch ethos," he muttered. "Ve vouldn't need vizards or creepy angels to enchant vings vor us ever again."

Curious, Zalith asked, "Can you still learn?"

Alucard sighed deeply. "I zon't know. I've 'eard zhat if vitches and mages aren't taught and trvained vrom certain age, is eizer impossible or too dangerous to try accessing zhe ethos later in life. And I've been alive vor centuries. Vor all ve know, if I tried, I could blow up an entire continent."

He sounded half serious and half sarcastic.

Zalith chuckled nervously. "So, Opus it is."

He sighed and rolled his eyes. "Vhatever. Do ve know vhere 'e is?"

"Our most recent intel tells us he's in Avalmoor," he said, glancing down at the report. "In a city called Crytharion… Aurivoss Lane."

"Vhat's 'e doing over zhere?"

"Settling… it would seem."

Alucard scoffed. "Vight. Vhen should ve go to 'im?"

"As soon as we can, I suppose," he said with a long sigh. "But what about the dragonlet?" he asked, looking down at the sleeping baby dragon in his lap.

"Ve could take 'er vith us," the vampire said as he got up and walked to the desk. "I zon't vink she vill vant to be levt 'ere vithout you."

"Will she be all right there? It's cold, isn't it?" he asked, glancing up at Alucard as he sat on the side of his desk.

He nodded. "I'm sure she vill be okay if she clings onto you again—you are like valking fire in zhe cold, no?" he said, smirking.

"That's true," Zalith said with an amused smile. "When should we go?"

"Zhat's up to you."

He exhaled deeply and leaned back in his seat as the dragonlet stirred in his lap. "I'd prefer to get this done today… but how long will it take to get there?"

"I can vly us zhere," he suggested. "Should only take… an hour or so."

"Are you sure you're okay to fly?" he asked worriedly.

"I'm okay," the vampire assured him. "Are *you* okay?"

He nodded and said, "I feel better now that I've had time to relax." His body felt better, but he was still admittedly a little on edge. He did his best to dismiss it and focus on the task at hand, though. "Should we bring food for the dragonlet?" he asked, looking down at her. "Just in case. She'll need to eat again at five, right?"

"Ve can do zhat. Ve can get Ezvin to prepare 'er next meal bevore ve go."

"Yeah," he agreed as he stood up, cradling the dragonlet in his arms. "I'm sure we'll have to provide Opus with collars for the animals. I'm fine with using some nice chains, though." He led the way to the door as Alucard followed.

"Ve can probably vind a pet store in Avalmoor. Crytharion is anozzer Voyal City; zhere vill be many expensive stores," he said, smiling—he looked *and* sounded excited.

Zalith smiled in response; he really loved seeing his fiancé happy. "Okay," he agreed, heading downstairs. "You can have some more blood if you need it," he then offered.

"I'll see 'ow I veel vhen ve get to Avalmoor."

"Okay, well, we should gear up," he said as they reached the bottom of the stairs. "I'm getting tired of surprises."

Alucard nodded. "I vill…go and get my vings. You can go and grab 'er vood, and zhen ve can meet in zhe 'all."

The demon nodded. "All right," he agreed.

He watched Alucard head towards the war room…and the fact that seeing him walk away *even in the safety of their own home* made him anxious…he felt so stupid. Embarrassed. He needed to get over all of this. It was behind them.

But the harrowing memories of his past wouldn't let him go free.

With a deep sigh, he looked down at the dragonlet, did his best to focus on her and what she needed, and then headed in the opposite direction from his fiancé. He'd see him again in a few minutes.

| **Alucard** |
| *Uzlia Isles, Usrul, Castle Reiner* |

First, Alucard strapped on his gun holsters, the leather snug against his sides. He drew both golden colts from the table, their weight familiar and reassuring, before sliding them into place. His blazer-like coat came next, the fabric settling over his shoulders as he buttoned it, hiding the gleam of the weapons from view. The holster-belt followed, buckled securely at his waist before he slid his rapier into its sheath with a quiet *click*. Finally, he took his cape from the back of the chair and swept it over his shoulders, the dark fabric settling into place.

He was ready.

But he didn't leave straight away. His gaze drifted across the cabinets, chests, and glass display cases lining the walls—an armoury built over four centuries of conflict.

Swords, revolvers, rifles, knives…each with its own history, each chosen in a different era when his methods shifted with the times. Avalmoor was a land of dragons and monsters twice a man's height; perhaps a sword wasn't the wisest choice today.

He crossed to the tall cabinet where his swords rested in orderly rows, opening it to return the rapier to its stand. His eyes moved over the collection—blades of every length and shape, steel polished to a mirror sheen, silver kept sharp despite its toxicity to him. The silver had its place; there were times when a werewolf needed killing.

At last, his attention settled on a short sword with a blackened blade, the metal dull rather than gleaming. Mortem-metallum, one of only two metals known to fatally wound a Numen and their offspring. Ideal for an Aegis. He took it from its stand, the weight sitting comfortably in his grip, then slid it into a sheath at his side.

The door then opened, and as he turned to face it, Alucard set his eyes on Zalith.

"Are you ready?" the demon asked.

He nodded.

"Could you hold her for a moment?" he then asked, walking to him as he held the baby dragon out—but when she realized that Zalith was trying to hand her off to Alucard, she hissed and climbed up onto his shoulder. "Never mind," he mumbled, reaching the table.

"Did you get 'er vood?"

"I did," he answered, taking his knife holster from the table. He attached it to his belt and sheathed his blade. "Could I perhaps have that gun again?" he asked, turning to face him.

Alucard frowned, convinced that Zalith despised guns, but he had no objections. "Uh…" he uttered, looking around—he could just give him one of his again— they *were* his best, after all. So, he unbuttoned his coat and took his left colt from its holster. "Maybe I should get you your own vone, no?" he asked, handing the weapon to Zalith.

"My own gun?" he asked, taking it from him.

"Yes…if you vanted—or two. Zhey are 'andy to 'ave."

The demon smiled. "I'd love that. Thank you," he said, tucking the gun into his belt.

"I can also make you a 'olster if you like; somevhere to keep zhem."

"It'll come in handy. Thank you."

Alucard smiled at him. He was certain there would be plenty of fur left from the dragon they'd slain today. Enough, at least, to finally make Zalith the fur-lined coat he'd been planning for some time, and a colt holster…perhaps a larger knife holster as well. Zalith owned no shortage of blades, and carrying more than one was simply practical. He'd see to it over the next week when he began work on his new combat attire.

"Vould you like anyving else?" he asked, taking Zalith's hand once he'd pulled his coat on.

"I'll take whatever you think I need."

The vampire smiled, looking around. "Vell...you zon't use swords, so...I vink you're covered vor now."

Zalith smirked, his tone low and suggestive as he murmured, "I know something else I need," closing the space between them.

Alucard was certain he knew what Zalith meant, but did he want that right now? He wasn't sure. "Vhat?" he asked quietly, trying to sift through the knot of feelings in his chest. Lately, whenever sex crossed his mind, reluctance followed. Not because he didn't want Zalith—he wanted him desperately, he loved being close to him more than anything—but the moment intimacy turned towards sex, nerves and embarrassment crept in.

He knew why. That disappointment from two weeks ago hadn't been a fleeting moment; it stayed, festering. Every time they'd been together lately, he couldn't make Zalith climax. Before, it hadn't weighed on him quite so heavily. Now, it sat like a stone in his gut. Zalith could undo him so effortlessly, but he couldn't seem to do the same in return, and the imbalance made him feel inadequate, like he was failing him. It wasn't just about sex; it was about what it made him feel. Incompetent. Ashamed. Not like a real man. And deep down, he knew that was more than the act—it was because he wasn't one. Not truly. Not male, not female. Just...something in-between, something he didn't fully understand. And if he couldn't even please the man he loved, what did that make him?

Zalith's seductive response came suddenly—"You," he said with a small smirk, his hand sliding to Alucard's waist before leaning in to press a slow kiss to his lips.

On the demon's shoulder, the dragonlet glowered at Alucard, as if she had any right to be jealous.

Alucard ignored her scowl, a faint smile tugging at his lips as he kissed Zalith back. Kissing was safe—kissing didn't make him hesitate. He released Zalith's hand, sliding his own to the demon's waist and pulling him a little closer, their lips moving together in slow, unhurried passes. With each kiss, the knot of uncertainty inside him loosened, replaced by a flicker of anticipation. And with his heat still lingering, that anticipation sharpened into a low, eager thrum. Maybe, *just maybe*, he was finally shaking off his hesitation. Maybe the self-disappointment didn't hold him as tightly as he'd feared—

A sharp sting tore him from the thought as the dragonlet lunged forward and bit his ear.

"*Căţea!*" he snapped frustratedly, his hand flying up to cover the sore spot as he stepped back to glare at her.

"Are you okay?" Zalith asked, his hand brushing lightly over Alucard's arm. He cupped his other palm gently over the dragonlet's eyes, blocking her view. The hiss cut off instantly. She melted under his touch, a soft, warbling coo escaping her as she leaned into his hand like it was the most comforting thing in the world. Her little body went limp against his chest, claws curling contentedly into the fabric of his shirt.

"No," Alucard complained, rubbing his ear.

"Let me see," he said, moving his hand to it—

"I'm vine," he mumbled and grabbed Zalith's wrist. He then glared at the dragonlet perched on the demon's shoulder, and as he did, she hissed at him.

Zalith frowned, looking at his wrist—Alucard was still holding it. Then, he looked at the vampire. "Okay," he said, pulling his wrist from; he sounded irritated—pissed off more like. "We should get going," he muttered.

That made Alucard feel anxious. "Vhat's vrong?" he asked.

"Nothing."

That was obviously a lie.

Frustration quickly outweighed the anxiety. "Zhen vhy do you seem mad?"

"I'm not mad. I'm just surprised you grabbed me like that."

Alucard's anxiety grew heavier. "I zidn't…mean to," he said apologetically. "I just took your vrist because I'm vine—you zon't need to vuss over me. I'm okay," he explained, taking Zalith's hand again—

The dragonlet hissed.

"Okay," Zalith replied. "We're going to have to find a way to teach her not to bite."

"I just zon't vink she likes me vor some veason. Maybe she can alveady tell I'm zhe anti-Numen or vhatever zhe fuck zhey call me," he grumbled.

"I think she's just trying to protect me. She doesn't seem bothered by you when we're not touching," the demon said, moving his hand away from the dragonlet as she settled down again, still perched on his shoulder.

"Maybe she vinks I'm trying to kill you."

"Maybe."

The vampire then sighed. "Should ve 'ead out?"

Zalith nodded. "Hopefully Opus is home," he said, leading the way to the door as Alucard followed.

"If 'e isn't, ve'll go and vind 'im."

When they reached the front door, Edwin called, "Sirs." They watched him cross the hall, and he stopped in front of them with a food-filled syringe. "For the baby," he said.

Alucard knew Zalith wasn't going to take it; he knew that he wouldn't want to put a food-filled syringe in his pocket. "Vank you," he said, taking it from Edwin and slipping it into his pocket.

With a humble bow, Edwin left.

Alucard then turned to Zalith. "Are you veady?" he asked as he opened the front door and followed his mate outside.

"I'm ready," the demon confirmed, stopping in the courtyard.

He didn't waste time. He moved his arms around Zalith despite the dragonlet's warning growl, and then he dematerialized into vermillion smoke.

It was time to return to one of the places Alucard hated most in the seven realms.

Chapter Eleven

Collars

| **Alucard** |

| *Avalmoor, Drakalyth Region, Crytharion City* |

Alucard landed and rematerialized on the snow-blanketed ground just shy of Crytharion's gates. The instant his boots touched down, a jagged pain lanced through his skull, rippling down his spine until every muscle in his body felt wrung with harrowing discomfort. His breath caught, teeth gritting against a groan—he refused to let Zalith hear it.

While the demon was busy steadying himself and checking on the dragonlet, Alucard drifted away, slipping to the shelter of a frost-coated tree and pressing his back against its trunk.

This wasn't new. He'd felt the drag of fatigue before—back in Atheson, when the weariness would creep in after a long day and blood would gradually banish it. But now… it clung to him no matter what he did, growing heavier each day, gnawing deeper. The blood only worked for so long before the weakness seeped back in, and now it had teeth—sharp, unrelenting pain that made him feel hollowed out.

Was it the heat? The thought gnawed at him. In this stage of his life, was he becoming more like Zalith, needing to sate his body's urges just to function? The idea unsettled him. He didn't know the answer, but he knew one thing for certain: something wasn't right; something in him was changing, and not for the better.

"Are you okay?" Zalith asked, standing beside him. "Do you want blood?"

Alucard exhaled deeply, resting his head against the tree as he shifted his gaze to his mate, who looked worried. The dragonlet, which was sitting on the demon's shoulder, glared at him, but he wasn't in the mood to compete with an animal right now. "I'll be okay," he tried to assure him, smiling through the lingering ache. "I just need a moment—is cold," he added, holding his cape tightly around himself.

"I can help warm you up…but you said you don't want me fussing over you," the demon mumbled.

He shook his head and moved closer to him. "You can varm me up."

Zalith unbuttoned his coat and ushered the baby dragon inside. Once she was comfortable—and hidden—he buttoned his coat up again, moved his arm around Alucard, and pulled him closer, rubbing his arm to try and help him get warm.

As his smile grew and the pain became distant enough to ignore, Alucard wrapped one arm around Zalith's waist and started leading the way forward.

"Hopefully we don't get spotted by someone who might cause trouble," the demon muttered as they reached the gates.

"I 'ave people 'ere. Zhey vouldn't let any of our enemies into zhe city, or anyvone who might know our enemies. Opus and 'is disgusting brover are zhe only exceptions—zhey're not our enemy…but zhey're not our vriends, eizer. Zhey are simply…tools vor us to use, no? Is also evening; most people vill be at 'ome or in zhe temples praying to Levoldus and zhe Aegis."

Zalith nodded. "What should we say to him about the payment he wanted for his first lot of services?" he asked quietly. "Getting a Lumendatt from Lilith."

Alucard hadn't shared his entire recollection with Zalith, had he? When they talked about his time in Djavhati, he remembered things. Lilith and Damien had possessed a Lumendatt at some point—that was the only way Lilith could have created all the scions she had stored in that chamber…and the only way she and Damien could have created their humanoid bodies. But they'd lost the crystals long ago because they'd started trying to use *his*.

"I zon't vink she even 'as vone anymore. Explains vhy she and Zamien vere trying to use mine, and vhy neizer of zhem can stay in zhis vorld vor very long—and 'onestly, probably vhy zhey're too scared to show zheir vaces and 'iding be'ind zheir cultists."

The demon frowned slightly. "Are you sure? What if she found another one?" he asked as they entered the snowy city and followed a sidewalk.

He shook his head. "Vrom vhat I've vemembered about 'er, she vould…use and sacrivice 'er scions vithout blinking. She 'asn't sent an army of zhem to vind us, vhich she normally vould, so she's likely conserving zhem; she 'as a limited number now."

Zalith nodded slowly, looking like he was pondering. "I hope that's true. If she can't create more of them, our goal to overpower their numbers might be a little easier."

Alucard hummed in agreement.

"As for Opus," the demon continued, "we could just tell him we're working on it."

"Vhat do ve do vhen ve kill Liliv? Everyvone vill know, and Opus vill come looking vor 'is payment."

The demon shrugged. "Lie and say someone else took it—or we can say we destroyed it."

Alucard laughed a little. "I zon't vink 'e vill believe us. Maybe ve should just get vid of 'im."

"Maybe. I have a feeling that'll just attract more people like him."

The vampire sighed, navigating the street—there weren't many people about, only those who looked like they had just left work and were on the way home, and the odd aristocrat here and there. "Maybe 'e vill lose intervest in zhe Lumendatt and set 'is eyes on a bigger prize if ve make 'im vait long enough."

"I hope so."

Alucard then set his eyes on a pet store up ahead: The Wyrm's Crown Pet Market. The place was still open despite the setting sun. "Should ve check zhere?"

"We can, but I don't think they're going to have what I'm looking for."

"Vhat are you looking vor?"

"Metal chain collars would be nice but considering they're going to wear them all the time, I want something higher end."

"Vell, if zhis place zoesn't 'ave vhat ve need, ve could 'ead up tovards zhe palace— is vhere all zhe aristocrats live," he said with a small smirk. "Maybe you vill vind vhat you're looking vor zhere."

"Maybe," the demon said. "I don't want to be here longer than we need to be, though."

"Okay, vell, ve can go up zhere, vind collars, and zhen go to vhere Opus is— Aurivoss Lane, vight? Is close to zhe palace."

Zalith nodded and asked, "Should we let him know we're dropping by?"

"And give 'im a chance to 'ide vhatever 'e might be up to?" Alucard replied with an amused smile. "No."

"I hope it's something good."

The vampire stopped outside The Wyrm's Crown Pet Market. "Is probably someving veird."

"I wouldn't be surprised," his mate said, and then he glanced at the store. "I don't think they're going to have anything here for the dragon. We might have to go to a jewellery store for her."

Alucard looked up and down the street, and when he set his eyes on Scaelith & Co. Jewellers with a glimmering sign in the window that unmissably informed the street that it was open later than most of its competitors, he nodded towards the store and said, "If you vant to 'ead over zhere and vind someving vor 'er, I could get collars vor Peaches and Sabazios in 'ere. Ve can meet outside bevore ve go to Opus; 'opevully ve can avoid needing to look in ozzer stores."

The demon smiled. "Okay. I'll meet you back here soon; I don't imagine I'll be too long." He leaned closer and kissed Alucard's lips, and then he turned around and headed towards the jewellery store.

Alucard watched him for a moment. His instincts urged him to go with him, both because he wanted to make sure that he was okay and because his body was pleading that he give in and let Zalith take him.

But he couldn't.

With a soft huff, he walked into the pet shop and tried focusing on what he was looking for.

| **Zalith** |
| ***Avalmoor, Drakalyth Region, Crytharion City, Scaelith & Co. Jewellers*** |

When he reached the jeweller's, the dragonlet fidgeted around inside Zalith's coat. He assumed she might be asking to come out for air, but he felt hesitant; he knew that dragons were a religious deity in Aegisguard, especially here in Avalmoor, and if people saw her, he'd get *a lot* of unwanted attention. However, she *was* very small, and if he let just her head and neck free, she'd pass as a snake or some other serpent.

Zalith undid the top button of his coat, allowing the baby dragon to poke her head out. She stretched her neck lazily, resting her chin on his collar as a soft, rhythmic purr rumbled against his chest. A small bell chimed as he pushed open the door, stepping into a world of glitter and gold.

Inside, the shop was nothing short of a treasure vault. Mahogany display cases lined the walls, their glass polished to a gleam so clear it was easy to forget it was there at all. Inside them, velvet cushions cradled bracelets, necklaces, and rings, some adorned with gems the size of a thumbnail, others with intricate engravings of coiling dragons, flame motifs, and curling clouds of gold filigree. A great chandelier hung from the high, domed ceiling, its tiers of cut crystal scattering light in a thousand little rainbows across the marble floor. Behind the counters, shelves and cabinets glittered with loose jewels—emeralds, sapphires, rubies, and topaz—some set in trays, others stored in delicate glass jars.

The scent of polished wood mingled with the faint tang of heated metal from a small goldsmith's bench in the back. Everywhere he looked, there was wealth—wealth tailored for the aristocracy that called this dragon-worshipping city home.

"Oh, hello, *aloha 'auinalā*! Welcome to Scaelith and Co. Jewellers," the owner greeted warmly, stepping out from behind one of the long counters; she had an accent that sounded *very* familiar, and so did what she just said. "I'm Leilani Scaelith, and my brothers, Kalani and Kekoa, are just working in the back." She was a trim woman in her late fifties, her hair swept up into an elegant spiral pinned with a comb shaped like a dragon's wing. Rings glittered on nearly every finger, each crowned with a jewel that caught the chandelier's light, and a heavy gold necklace studded with sapphires rested against the high lace collar of her gown. As she drew closer, her eyes widened, her words faltering, "Oh, my… what a darling… what is that?" she asked, her gaze fixed on the tiny creature nestled in his coat.

Zalith smiled pleasantly. "You wouldn't believe me if I told you," he replied. "But thank you." And then he chuckled lightly. "I recognize your accent. Is it Maluhian?"

"It is," Leilani said contently. "You've visited?"

"My fiancé and I took a short vacation to A'okalani Cove Resort recently."

"Oh, a beautiful place. Lots of wildlife to enjoy."

"We ended up helping this tortoise—well, it was mostly my fiancé," he told her, smiling fondly at the recent memory. "It was covered in gemstones."

Her eyes lit up brighter. "Aniani tortoises." She sighed softly. "Poor little things. They're hunted something awful." Her smile returned as she rolled her shoulders. "What are you looking for today? We have a very wide range."

"I'm interested in a bracelet for a baby—something for a newborn."

"Of course," Leilani beamed, curiosity still flickering in her eyes. "This way."

He followed her to a display case near the front of the shop. Here, the designs were smaller and simpler: thin chains of silver and gold, plain bands with only a token gemstone, and modest dragon engravings. If Zalith had to guess, these were meant for the less fortunate citizens of Crytharion, far from the dazzling finery behind the cases reserved for nobility.

"We have gold and silver—we even have some made of platinum," she smiled, pointing at the display.

He thought to himself for a moment. At first, he thought gold was a good choice, but he remembered what Alucard said about it being toxic to dragons, so that wasn't a good idea. He couldn't get silver because that was harmful to Alucard, and platinum was poisonous to Lethidian demons, and since the dragonlet was an Aegis—or at the very least the offspring of one—he was sure that the metal would hurt her. He wasn't going to settle for steel, though.

"Do you sell anything…" he paused, asking himself whether the word might have spread beyond his and Alucard's circles yet, "…Arcanean?"

Leilani's brows lifted, the surprise in her face tempered by something else—interest, maybe even respect.

"I'm looking for something very resilient," he added smoothly. "You know how babies are."

She gave a soft, knowing laugh. "Well, that's a word one doesn't hear very often at all." Her tone lowered a fraction, almost conspiratorial, and she glanced towards the shopfront, eyes flicking left and right as if to check whether anyone had lingered too close. "Come with me."

Leilani led him away from the display cases of gold and gemstone trinkets and to a tall, dragon-carved bookcase along the far wall. From a distance, it appeared purely decorative, laden with heavy leather-bound tomes and ornate curios. But when she pressed her hand against the spine of one thick volume, the shelf clicked and swung inward on a hidden hinge, revealing a narrow passage lit by soft amber lanterns.

"Discretion is key, sir," she murmured, stepping inside first.

The hidden room beyond was small but lavish, its walls lined with glass cabinets and velvet-layered shelves. Here were the treasures that never saw the main shop floor: rings that shimmered faintly with protective wards, pendants forged of rare Arcana metals that caught the light with an otherworldly gleam, and bracelets that seemed to hum with a subtle, contained energy.

"These," Leilani said, gesturing towards a cabinet in the centre, "are the pieces reserved for those who understand their worth—and their danger." Her eyes clearly examined him for a moment. "If you're looking for demon artifacts, we have a case just over there," she told him, gesturing to the back wall. "Feel free to look around. If you need help finding anything, or if you don't see what you're seeking, let me know, and I'll help as best I can."

"Thank you."

She gave him another smile before heading over to the door, where she then stood and waited.

Zalith moved slowly through the hidden room, his boots sinking almost soundlessly into the thick, wine-red carpet. The air felt heavier, as if steeped in the residue of centuries-old enchantments. Every shelf along the walls glittered with restrained power; rings with stones seemed to shift in colour when viewed from a different angle, pendants holding tiny vials of glowing liquid, and knives with edges that shimmered faintly as though alive with heat.

One display held fragile silver circlets traced with runes so fine that they could almost be mistaken for cracks in the metal. Another was lined with bracelets of deep obsidian, each carved into scales realistic enough that he could almost swear they moved when he looked directly at them. A narrow case beside it contained brooches shaped like dragons mid-flight, their eyes two pinpricks of emerald or sapphire light.

He paused here and there, leaning over to better examine an engraved sigil or to watch a gemstone catch and fracture the lamplight into crimson shards. But then his attention shifted. Against the back wall, near a softly glowing lantern, stood a long cabinet filled with jewellery unlike any of the others. Crafted from a gold-toned metal that held an unmistakable crimson sheen, as though the metal itself had been tempered in blood and flame. Rings, chains, pendants, bracelets, and even small etched plaques gleamed beneath the glass, every edge catching the warm red glimmer. Something about it drew him forward.

And his eyes landed on exactly what he was looking for. A baby bracelet.

"What's this?" he asked, looking over his shoulder at Leilani.

She walked over. "Oh, that's vendite. It's a *very* rare and equally expensive metal. It is extremely powerful. Elves use it a lot in their own jewellery making." She pressed her finger against the keyhole—or what looked like one, anyway—and the case clicked open. "It is *much* better at repelling ethos than silver, but curiously, it can also be used to *amplify* certain Arcana, like enchantments. From what I know, though, only elves and mages are capable of applying enchantments, and the metal is often exclusive to the royal bloodlines." She smiled proudly as she slowly lifted the lid. "I can't mention my suppliers, but let's just say that they know an elf who knows another elf." She waved her hand over the displayed jewellery, and it shimmered that beautiful crimson again. "None of our competitors come close. It's simply the best you can buy."

That was what he wanted, the best he could get, and vendite sounded perfect. It also *looked* perfect, and it made him want more than just pet collars. "Do you have more?" he asked her. "I'm also looking for a ring and a chain—like this," he said, reaching beneath his shirt and pulling out his thin gold chain.

A devious smile appeared on Leilani's face. "Oh, of course we do. Though…I'm very sorry, I don't mean to be disrespectful *at all*—it's just the store policy—but can you afford it? It really is quite expensive, and only our royal elven clientele has the money."

He smiled, aggravated. "Do you often say these things to your customers?"

Leilani frowned, looking slightly tense now. "Oh, well…I have to make sure before I take it out above the protective ward. One can never truly be too careful, not after what happened with Miss Judy." She paused briefly, shaking her head as she gestured to the doorway. "Across the street, Mrs Judy's Engagement Supplies, a man dressed in robes that belonged to a respected mage gathering here in the city asked her to take one of her biggest diamond rings from its case so that he could see, and he took off with it!" she exclaimed and then huffed. "My brothers have been very insistent since then that we don't risk ending up like poor Mrs Judy," she added, shaking her head. "Do you have some identification? Or perhaps you could show me you have enough to buy this?"

Zalith sighed, trying to maintain his patience. He didn't want to upset her; she was just doing her job. But he'd be lying if he told himself that he wasn't bothered by all of this. "I don't have any identification," he told her—and among everything else he was already feeling and thinking, that fact reminded him that IDs were something he and Alucard needed to get, and so did everyone else who worked for them. That was something to think about later, though. He dismissed the thought and continued kindly, "You should hire some security or invest in some anti-theft devices."

She nodded stiffly, seeming hesitant. "Yes, you're right. My brothers are just very hard to convince." She then frowned apologetically. "I really am sorry."

With another sigh, he reached into his pocket and into his vault; he grabbed a wad of coronam notes, and then he pulled them out, showing them to her. "Is this proof enough?"

"Um…well—"

Another sigh, another reach into his vault. This time, he took out several pieces of paper—cidaris notes, equivalent to *a million dollars* in Eltaria. Surely, that must be enough.

Leilani looked embarrassed at this point. "Okay, that's fine. I'm so, so sorry." Perhaps it was shame, actually. "My brothers, you see."

"I understand," he muttered, slipping the papers and notes back into his vault.

She cleared her throat and said, "We have a lot more vendite in the repository. If you're fine with heading down a narrow staircase, I can take you."

He nodded. "Lead the way."

| Alucard |

| *Avalmoor, Drakalyth Region, Crytharion City, The Wyrm's Crown Pet Market* |

Alucard was finishing paying for the collars he'd got for Peaches and Sabazios. He wasn't sure if Zalith was waiting for him—he'd been a while, but he wanted to make sure he got the best he possibly could for his animals.

Alucard was *still* waiting to pay for the collars he'd chosen for Peaches and Sabazios, standing behind a customer who had been planted at the counter for what felt like an eternity. The man—a wiry guy in a threadbare wool coat and a bowler hat with a frayed brim—had been talking the shop owner's ear off for at least ten minutes.

At first, the conversation was nothing but droning small talk: the price of coal this winter, the mayor's wife fainting at the theatre, and a neighbour's scandalous affair with the stablemaster's apprentice. Utterly unremarkable gossip that Alucard could have happily gone another four centuries without overhearing.

He shifted his weight and glanced at the collars in his hands, reminding himself that Zalith might be waiting—

The sudden change in the man's tone caught his attention.

The guy leaned in closer to the shopkeeper, lowering his voice as he asked, "And that shipment…?"

And the owner's reply was careless, as if such talk was perfectly ordinary in this city. "It arrived this morning. Came in with the fish barrels. She's being processed now."

Alucard's attention sharpened. Processed?

The man's next words made his stomach turn.

"Good. Make sure the horns are pulled clean this time; the last one I bought still had the fucking bases attached. Fur, too; the finer it's cut, the better the price."

The owner chuckled as if it were all part of the day's business. "Don't worry. You'll have your hide by week's end."

Alucard's jaw tightened, nausea rising in his throat. He knew what they were talking about. It was no secret that humans hunted, sold, and smuggled Arcana beasts all around the world. These people slaughtered those poor animals for parts, some even did it for fun. And it wasn't just the cruelty that turned his stomach, but the casualness of it, the way they discussed the killing as though they were talking about trimming a horse's mane.

He stared at the back of the man's head, willing himself not to say anything. Killing anyone in this city wouldn't go unnoticed, and he'd be risking starting a battle that he and Zalith really didn't need right now. But every part of him wanted to put the man through the same 'processing' he'd just so flippantly described.

The best he could do at the moment was save that animal. So he reached out to the vampires positioned in the nearby mountains. He told them to search this place and find the Arcana beast or beasts being slaughtered here.

"All right, catch you tomorrow morning," the man said to the owner.

"Later, Bert," the owner replied.

The man then took the bag of pet food and left the store.

Alucard put the pet collars on the counter, clenching his other fist at his side. How *badly* he wanted to grab the man and break his frail little neck.

"Just these?" he asked, grabbing a paper bag.

He nodded.

The man put them into the bag and said, "Two gold, three silver, and five bronze, please."

Alucard reached into his pocket and his vault. He couldn't touch the silver coins, so he just took out three gold ones.

"You got anything smaller? I don't have enough bronze."

The vampire huffed irritably through his nose and glanced around. He snatched a small bag of cat treats, bringing the total to three gold.

"All right," the owner muttered, putting the treats into the bag. "Here—"

Alucard snatched the bag before the man could push it all the way to him. He then turned and headed for the door.

"You got a problem?" the man called.

Ignoring him, Alucard left the store and huffed again, harder this time. He knew that his vampires would do their job, but he couldn't stop thinking about the poor animals that had died under that man's shop.

Zalith wasn't waiting outside.

The street was busier than it was before he went in, and all the noise was becoming overwhelming. He did his best to ignore it, though, and leaned against the wall, staring through the crowds at the jewellery store sitting at the end of the road.

He lingered outside, the bustle of the street pressing in on him from every side. People passed in an endless stream, muttering to one another beneath the muffled hiss of falling snow. Their voices blurred together, a constant low murmur that only deepened the restless edge in his chest. He couldn't shake the sour taste the shop left in his mouth— the image of that Arcana beast, alive one moment, gutted the next, clung to him like a foul stench.

The cold bit sharper with every minute. He drew his cape tighter around his shoulders, frowning into the wind. The sooner they left this city, the better. But what was taking Zalith so long? His first instinct was to go and find him, to duck into the jewellery shop, step out of the cold, and lose himself in the sight of his mate's face. Even just the thought of Zalith, his comforting presence, and that unshakable confidence loosened the tightness in his chest. He knew that if he saw him now, even for a second, the rage would dull.

He straightened, deciding he might do exactly that—until his gaze caught on a single face in the sea of strangers.

For a moment, the world seemed to still.

Through the crowd, a pair of eyes as red as fresh blood locked with his own icy stare. Recognition hit him like a blade to the ribs—harsh, unbidden, and absolute. The face was harrowingly familiar, carved deep into memory, and it was looking straight at him with nothing but pure, cutting malice—

"How did it go?" Zalith asked.

Alucard snapped out of it, turning his head to see Zalith. But he could have sworn…. He turned his head, staring back into the crowd, but who he thought he'd seen was nowhere. He frowned, setting his eyes back on his mate, trying to find his voice.

"What did you buy?" the demon asked.

He frowned. "Vhat?"

"You look guilty."

His frown thickened. "Vhat?" he asked again. But then he reached into the paper bag and took out the two chain collars. "I got zhese."

Zalith took them and asked, "What else?"

"Noving," he mumbled.

"Then why are you making that face?"

"Vhat vace?"

With a skeptical frown, Zalith started patting him down.

"I zon't 'ave anyving," he mumbled.

The demon stepped back and eyed him for a moment…but he soon lost his suspicious stare. "Okay…" he said, dragging out the word as he shifted his attention to the collars.

Holding his cape shut to keep the cold out, Alucard sighed and asked, "Do you like zhem?"

"I do. Are you sure this is big enough for Sabazios?" He held up the larger chain.

Alucard nodded. "'E von't get any bigger zhan 'e is now."

"Okay," he said, handing the collars back to him.

Alucard put them in his coat pocket along with the cat treats.

"I got this for you." Zalith held out a small box and opened it, revealing a gold ring. "It's vendite. I'm going to get Opus to enchant this for you to wear instead of the gold ring since it's toxic to her," he said, glancing at the dragonlet, which was sleeping in his coat with her head resting on his collar.

Taking it from him, Alucard smiled. "Vank you…but I like zhe vone you alveady gave me—your vather's ving."

The demon smiled, too. "I know, I just thought it would be nice to have something extra. You don't even have to wear it; I thought it might make her a little less mean to you," he said, looking down at the dragon again.

Tucking the ring in his pocket, Alucard's smile grew. "She is growing on you, no?"

Zalith shrugged. "I just want everyone to be happy."

Alucard took hold of his hand. "Vell, vank you. I 'ave plenty of spare vingers vor."

The demon then laughed quietly. "I think I might have been a little rude to the jeweller," he said as they walked up the street.

"Vhy?"

"She didn't think I could afford what I bought."

The vampire scoffed. "I assume she vas speechless vhen you proved 'er vrong?"

"I almost felt like she was going to ask me to leave or call her brothers to come and frisk me."

Alucard laughed. "You must 'ave veally upset 'er."

Zalith shrugged. "I suggested that she hire some security. Hopefully she'll take my advice and not learn the hard way when someone is actually there to steal."

He nodded, and then he grumbled, "Vell, *I*'ope zhat Opus and 'is brover 'ave learned zheir lesson. I zon't 'ave zhe patience vor zhem today."

The demon sighed deeply. "I hope so, too."

Chapter Twelve

— ⸲ ✝ ⸴ —

Unfavourable Angels

| Alucard |

| *Avalmoor, Drakalyth Region, Crytharion City* |

Aurivoss Lane was narrow, flanked by crooked iron lamp-posts and buildings of soot-darkened stone, their tall chimneys coughing faint ribbons of smoke into the icy evening air. Dragon-headed gargoyles jutted from cornices and rooftops, their glassy eyes catching flashes of lamplight as carriages clattered past. Snow gathered in the gutters and along the ridged iron fences, muting the city's usual noise beneath a frozen hush.

Once they reached Opus' house, Alucard and Zalith stepped up onto the narrow porch, the wood creaking beneath their boots. The townhouse was tall and lean like its neighbours, its green-painted door flanked by twisted columns carved with dragon-scale motifs, their once-gilded details dulled by weather and time.

Alucard raised his hand and knocked twice, glancing at Zalith, who looked hesitant. He knew his mate was thinking the same thing, hoping that this went smoothly, that Opus and his brothers wouldn't aggravate either of them. The last thing they needed right now was a confrontation.

When the door opened, a butler dressed in *pink* and holding a purple, yellow-striped teapot in his right hand greeted them. "Good evening, sirs," he said—he didn't just sound physically tired but perhaps tired of his life as a whole; the bags under his eyes were so black one might mistake them for small lumps of coal. "Can I help you?"

Alucard couldn't help but smirk amusedly.

"We're here to see Opus—Magnus," Zalith answered.

"Do you have an appointment?" he asked tonelessly.

"Yes."

"Name and time?"

Alucard glanced at Zalith. He was searching the butler's mind.

"Gerald White, five o'clock," his mate then said.

Looking him up and down, the butler nodded. "Yes…your wife gnawed off your…privates with…" he paused and took out a piece of paper… "with her three wooden prosthetic teeth which she deliberately filed and sharpened because you were having an affair with a Mrs Cherry…Cherry Pie, the strumpet from Frosteath Farmstead. *That* Gerald White?"

"Unfortunately," Zalith confirmed with a smile.

"Right…and this is?" he questioned, looking at Alucard.

"Why? Are you interested?" he asked with a smirk.

The butler kept his vacant stare. "Magnus prefers to see his patients alone."

Zalith frowned. "Well, I can't go in alone. I have anxiety and get very shy," he lied, still smirking.

The butler eyed them both for a moment. "Sure," he mumbled and stepped aside. "Come in."

Alucard and Zalith stepped into the house.

"This way," the man said after closing the front door. "Wait in here until Magnus is ready," he told them, taking them down the hall to another room. "He will be with you shortly."

Nodding, Zalith led the way into what looked to be Opus' office.

The butler then pulled the door shut, leaving them alone.

"Who makes zheir butler vear pink?" Alucard asked with a scoff, slumping down on the couch.

Zalith laughed as he sat on the arm beside him. "Maybe so they can see him from really far away."

"Maybe," he grumbled.

They didn't have much time to talk. Just moments later, the door to the left of the desk opened.

Opus entered, nose buried in a chart. "Hmm…Mr Gerald again. That makes a third occurrence this month…" his voice trailed as he lifted his gaze to find them standing there. "Ah," he said coolly, his expression dimming with displeasure. He set the chart down and leaned one hand against the edge of his desk, the other slipping into his coat pocket. "I should like to feign surprise…but alas, I find myself entirely unshocked. Dare I ask to what I owe the honour of this unannounced visitation?"

Alucard scowled at him. What the fuck was that ridiculous accent? He wasn't entirely surprised, though. Angels were like children; they changed depending on their surroundings, they listened to those around them and adopted their way of speaking. Opus had clearly been socializing with the aristocrats and socialites of this city—he sounded just like them.

"We need you to enchant some more items for us," the demon said, standing up.

Opus gave a short, derisive scoff as he straightened his posture. "And tell me, have you come bearing what I requested in recompense for my prior assistance, or am I once again expected to extend charity unreciprocated?"

"We're working on it," Zalith lied. "I'm sure you know as well as we do that killing a Numen is no easy task."

Opus offered a cool smile as he settled behind his desk. "On the contrary. You presented yourself as a man of singular capability—indeed, I was under the distinct impression you *excelled* at such things. It appears I may have rather grossly overestimated your aptitude."

"Ve're vorking on," Alucard snarled, silencing him. "You could just as easily acquire a Lumendatt vrom ozzer sources—you zon't need to vely on us."

He didn't miss a beat as he began leafing through a stack of paperwork. "Oh, but I *wish* to rely on you. You and your companion strike me as such…*ambitious* creatures. I find it endlessly diverting to reap the fruits of another's struggle. So, once you've acquired what I've requested, we may then discuss further arrangements. Yes?"

Alucard was growing impatient faster than usual, likely because of how smug this asshole was being. Still, as he sat up straight when Zalith sat beside him again, he did his best to keep the aggravation restrained. "Vell, is Zaliv who owes you vor zhat, not me," he said, eager to get this over with. "*I* am 'ere to ask vor your services."

Opus studied him a moment longer before a languid smile curved across his lips. He rose, circled to the front of his desk, and leaned against its edge with all the ease of a man thoroughly entertained. "Quite so…. It was Zalith who came to me in desperation all those years ago, pleading for aid. And it was I who graciously imbued that rather elegant ring upon your hand," he remarked, giving the jewellery a pointed glance. "So, do enlighten me. What might a Disavowed creature of your…pedigree require of one such as myself? A figure of some standing, you understand." He gave a theatrical sigh. "If you're here to inquire about wings, I'm afraid you've knocked at the wrong door entirely—"

Alucard sprang out of his seat before Zalith could say whatever he was going to say to match the furious look on his face; the vampire snatched Opus' throat and glared into his eyes as he stared back in startle. And he snarled…but he hesitated. This sudden burst of anger—it wasn't like him, it wasn't how he usually reacted when someone drew attention to his scars. But he wasn't going to lose his composure in front of this revolting little man; that would just amuse him. "Choose your next vords visely, or I vill vemove your ability to speak," he warned him.

Opus clutched the edge of the desk behind him, wide-eyed. "Y-yes. My deepest apologies," he choked out.

The vampire let go of his neck and stepped back, watching Opus straighten his white waistcoat, smooth his silvery hair, and clear his throat with injured dignity.

"My sincerest apologies," the angel repeated, his voice thinned with humiliation. "Now then…how may I be of service to you?" He blinked slowly. "Perhaps anger manageme—"

Alucard struck him backhanded. Opus hit the floor with a thud, and the vampire exhaled through his nose in a quiet, irritable snarl. The moment was brief, but it didn't settle anything. If anything, the anger only sharpened. The simmering fury was rising fast, coiling tight beneath his skin. Maybe this wasn't the right time to try reasoning with anyone. Maybe he wasn't in the right state to even try.

But that man and his brothers pissed him off worse than anyone else. Was it because of the way they looked at him? The way they made him feel less than demon, less than noble, less than *worthy*. It infuriated him.

Or maybe it wasn't just them. Maybe it was everything. The exhaustion. The frustration. The confusion that had morphed into a deep, dismaying feeling of inferiority. Perhaps it was his heat, the relentless pull of it and the way it made him crave Zalith's touch even as he kept himself from giving in, even as the truth and reality of who he was and what he wasn't capable of gnawed at him. The ache of wanting, the shame of not knowing how to want it properly. It was all of it. Pressing down. Pressing in.

And he was so very tired of pretending it wasn't.

Opus grunted as he climbed to his feet.

Alucard rolled his eyes.

"Well…" the angel muttered, dabbing at the blood on his lip with a lace-edged handkerchief, "one cannot help but detect that *distinctive* stench about you." His eyes lifted, cold and gleaming. "All that simmering frustration—such a shame, truly. Were you graced with the attentions of a female, I daresay it would be remedied in short order." He offered a thin, blood-streaked smile, smug despite his position on the floor.

Alucard moved again, his hand snapping forward—

But Opus scrambled back, palms raised in protest. "Come now," he said breathlessly, still clutching his handkerchief. "Let us not descend into further violence, yes? I should think I've been quite thoroughly chastised for one evening."

"Perhaps it would be best if you listened rather than spoke," Zalith called from where he was sitting, clearly enjoying the show; he had that amused gleam about his face.

Opus gave Zalith a narrowed glance before turning his gaze—reluctantly—back to Alucard. With a tight breath, he straightened his cuffs and returned to his chair behind the desk. "My services, then," he said, voice clipped but composed. "Do tell, what is it you require of me, exactly?"

Alucard pulled the chain collars from his coat pocket and placed them on Opus' desk, followed by the ring Zalith had gifted him. As he laid it down, Zalith stepped forward, presenting a delicate gold chain—similar to his current one—and a small, ornate baby bracelet. "You vill enchant all of zhese to 'ide zhe vearer vrom zhe Numen."

The angel examined the collection with a faint frown, fingertips brushing the surface of one collar. "My, my… quite the assortment. This shall require no small effort, I assure you."

"Zhen get to," Alucard snarled.

He folded his hands, leaning back slightly with a composed smile. "Not until we have come to an agreement on compensation, yes."

"Zhe fuck do you vant?" he snapped angrily.

Opus looked up at them both, the corner of his mouth twitching. "Tell me, what *else* might you offer, aside from coin, yes? This world's currency holds little value to me, I'm afraid."

"What do you want?" Zalith asked.

The angel offered a smile. "My brother still nurses a rather persistent fondness for your company. His proposal remains, shall we say, open."

"And I've made my stance on that perfectly clear," Zalith replied, placing a steadying hand against Alucard's chest before the vampire could lunge for Opus again.

Opus leaned back in his chair with a theatrical sigh, fingertips steepled. "A dreadful pity, truly. He does so hate rejection."

"Just tell us vhat zhe fuck you vant," Alucard snapped, his patience fraying.

Opus tilted his head with a sly smile and turned his attention to Zalith. "What, pray tell, are you concealing beneath that fine coat of yours, yes?"

"That's between me and what's in my coat," the demon answered dryly.

Alucard let out a quiet, amused hum.

Opus leaned back in his chair, lacing his fingers together. "I see…. Well then." His smile sharpened. "I still desire a measure of his blood," he said, nodding towards Alucard. "The offer stands."

The vampire frowned. "Vhat?"

"No," Zalith refused.

Alucard scowled. How could he have forgotten? Zalith had told him while they were on the run that Opus asked for a sample of his blood so that he could understand how vampires were made.

Opus' expression soured. "Then I daresay our conversation has reached its natural end. I require only select commodities, and if you are incapable of furnishing any of them, I must kindly insist you take your leave, yes."

"Surely, there's something else," Zalith said. "Do you need someone taken care of, perhaps? Or, if business is slow, we can hire a few women to seduce some new clients and chew their man parts off for you," he suggested, smirking.

A displeased wrinkle formed between his brows. "You may fancy yourself amusing, sir, but I assure you, the humour is entirely lost on me."

"I vink 'e's vunny," Alucard said.

Opus turned his gaze towards the vampire, eyes narrowing with interest. "What of your venom, yes? Might I be permitted to study it? I've yet to examine a specimen from one with Numen lineage."

Alucard tensed uncomfortably. "Is no divverent vrom any ozzer zemon's—"

Opus gave a knowing smile. "I rather doubt that, my dear boy."

"No," Zalith denied. "You're not studying any part of him."

The angel turned his gaze to Zalith, his tone light, almost teasing, as he asked, "Must you keep him all to yourself, dear demon?"

"Because he's mine," Zalith said firmly.

Opus smiled thinly. "For the time being."

"What the fuck is that supposed to mean?" Zalith snarled.

Alucard rolled his eyes. He knew what Opus was about to say.

Opus gave a languid shrug. "Merely an observation, yes. Once, he was the property of the Diabolus. Then he passed to Lilith and Damien. Then Damien alone. And now, he is yours. One must wonder…how long before someone else claims him?"

The vampire sighed. This wasn't the first time he'd heard people talking about him as if he were a tool. To most, that's what he was, a weapon for killing Numen, a weapon to steal from someone. But he knew that wasn't how Zalith saw him, and he'd heard this so many times that he felt no need to fight.

"Are you threatening me, Opus?" Zalith asked tonelessly.

The angel smiled, unbothered. "Heavens, no. Merely making conversation, yes." He then turned his attention to Alucard, voice lilting with false politeness, "Might I request a sample of your venom?"

"No," Alucard replied with a sharp snarl.

"We're your clients, Opus. Would you make Gerald White do some strange little task for you in lieu of money?"

"My clients are not six-hundred-year-old demons, nor the offspring of a Numen, yes. You two possess far more…valuable commodities. But, as this appears unlikely to progress in any favourable direction, allow me to offer a compromise." He adjusted his cuffs and rested his arms on the desk. "There are certain supplies I find myself in need of—items not easily acquired through conventional means, especially since that little virus I saved you from managed to spread from Nefastus—supply lines have been cut off, you see. Fetch for me the blood of an arachnoid queen, and a snow fiend's egg. Do so, and I shall enchant these trinkets for you, yes," he added with a nod towards the collars and jewellery. "Or, if you prefer, I shall begin the work while you're off retrieving what I require. Convenient for all parties, I should think."

Zalith took his eyes off Opus and looked at Alucard—clearly, he didn't know what either of those were.

Alucard sighed and said to Opus, "Vine."

"Splendid," Opus replied, folding his hands. "I shall await your return with great anticipation."

Zalith took Alucard's hand and wordlessly headed for the door.

The vampire followed just as silently. The sooner they left this place, the better.

| Zalith |

| *Avalmoor, Drakalyth Region, Crytharion City* |

Zalith rolled his as he pulled Alucard through the house, headed for the front door. Aggravated didn't do justice in explaining how he felt right now. He didn't want to have to do this. Slaving around for Opus was humiliating, and he was considering whether they even needed his services… but the answer was yes. They needed him to enchant those chains and jewellery so that they could remain safe and hidden from the Numen.

He hated that it had to be Opus, though.

That angel wasn't the only thing he couldn't dismiss, though. Alucard seemed angrier than usual; it wasn't like him to react so volatile, and he'd been with his fiancé long enough to know that he often retreated behind a vacant stare when someone insulted his place in demon society—he never attacked like he just had.

Zalith couldn't help but wonder—he couldn't help but *worry*. Was something going on with Alucard? Of course, it could just be the fact that he was still in heat. He remembered how it felt; he'd been through it enough times. It made him feel frustrated most of the time, and often, that frustration became anger. That was probably it.

He glanced at Alucard. There was no sign of his anger now. He looked tired, if anything.

The demon opened his mouth to speak—

"Well, well…" came that unmistakably grating voice. "I daresay I knew you'd come crawling back."

They both halted, turning their eyes over their shoulders—

Of course. It was him.

Ulric was leaning languidly against a side table, a glass of white wine dangling from his hand, his posture as careless as the smirk stretched across his face. He'd just emerged from the door to its left, the faint scent of expensive cologne and wine-soaked breath trailing after him. "It's been an age," he drawled, voice syrupy with drink as he stumbled a step forward. "Well—one month, perhaps two? I've quite lost count." He gave a lazy, crooked grin as he came to stand before them. "Tell me… couldn't bear the distance, hm? Thought you'd come bask in my company once more?"

Alucard scowled, but he didn't speak. Instead, he looked at Zalith.

Zalith wasn't going to be rude, but he didn't want to upset Alucard, either—nor did he want to be here any longer than he had to be. So, he smiled pleasantly and asked Ulric, "How have you been?"

Ulric gave a lazy shrug, swirling his wine before taking a sip. "Oh, you know… enduring. Magnus insists we reside in this frigid mausoleum. The man has taste, yes, but comfort? Absolutely not. I've half a mind to set the drapes alight just for warmth."

The demon let out a polite laugh. "He's quite stubborn, isn't he?"

He scoffed, glancing around the grand, draughty corridor. "Stubborn? My dear, that's putting it kindly. He'd sooner let the frost take him than concede an inch of pride. It's like living with a particularly well-dressed glacier."

"Well, what can you do? He's family," Zalith said with a shrug. Then he turned slightly, gesturing back towards the front door. "Anyway, we were just leaving, so enjoy your evening—"

"Now, now, hold a moment," Ulric interrupted, setting his glass down. "Why the rush?" he asked, his words just shy of a slur.

"Ve 'ave vings to do," Alucard muttered, clearly unamused.

Ulric grinned, stepping forward, his gaze fixed on Zalith like a wolf scenting prey. "Mm… yes, yes, I'm sure. But what harm is there in a brief reprieve?" he purred. "Come, sit by the fire, let the cold wait a little longer. We've fine wine, decent company…." He leaned in slightly, voice dropping. "And I daresay you could use the warmth."

"Maybe some other time," Zalith refused. "But thank you." Then, he turned around and headed for the door as Alucard followed.

But Ulric seemed incapable of accepting rejection. "Oh, come now," he called, trailing after them. "I could show you a far finer evening than whatever sordid plans you've got in mind with—"

The moment his hand brushed Zalith's shoulder, Alucard spun on him and slammed him back against the wall. "'E said no," the vampire hissed, his voice low and dangerous.

Zalith chuckled softly behind him, his amusement plain. There was something deeply satisfying about watching Alucard grow protective and *possessive*. It aroused him, and the moment he got a chance, he'd let the anticipation and desire enthral him.

Ulric scoffed, writhing in the vampire's grip but too clumsy to break free. "Tch. I've no doubt that if *you* weren't here, sullying the place with your stench, he might have had a rather different answer."

"If I veren't 'ere, 'e'd be telling you zhe same ving. Fuck off bevore zhis becomes a much more unvavourable situation vor you."

The angel cast a fleeting glance at Zalith, and then he fixed a simmering glare on Alucard. A slow, crooked smile spread across his face as he ceased struggling and raised both hands in theatrical surrender. "Very well," he said smoothly, voice low and oily. "No need to be *uncivilized*."

Alucard gave a final irritated snarl before releasing him and stepping back, taking Zalith's hand in his own.

Ulric dusted off the front of his blazer, straightening it with a huff. "It was merely a jest," he said with a short, brittle scoff. "Good-natured. Harmless." His gaze flicked once more to Zalith. "Friendly."

"Ve're not your vriends," Alucard snapped coldly.

Ulric's grunt came sharp and graceless, the sting of rejection barely masked.

Alucard turned without another word, tugging Zalith with him towards the front door. The conversation was over.

Ulric was left with nothing but the echo of their exit.

Chapter Thirteen

Rest

| **Alucard** |
| *Avalmoor, Drakalyth Region, Crytharion City* |

Leaving that house brought no relief. The anger clung to Alucard like damp smoke, thick and impossible to shake. He could still feel the phantom heat of his palm from where it had struck Opus. He wanted to kill those arrogant angels; he wanted to tear the smirks off their faces with his teeth. But starting another war wasn't worth the blood, not when he and Zalith were already exhausted from the current one.

They walked through the gloomy city in silence, boots tapping over the glistening cobbles. Light, icy drizzle freckled their coats, and the lamps overhead flickered with a sickly yellow glow. Alucard glanced at Zalith beside him, watching the way he gently adjusted the dragonlet nestled against his chest, tucking her deeper into the warmth of his coat before fastening it closed.

A second later, Zalith seized his hand and pulled him into the shadows of a nearby alley.

Alucard grunted lightly as his back met the cool brick, white stone slick with rain. The demon pressed in close, hands caging him in, and the fury knotting Alucard's ribs softened under the heat of that familiar closeness.

"You're so grumpy today," Zalith murmured, smirking as his breath ghosted over Alucard's lips.

The vampire huffed. "I 'ate zhose angels," he muttered.

"I know, baby," Zalith murmured. He slid his hand up to Alucard's neck, his thumb stroking slow, lazy circles just beneath his jaw. "I hate them too. But I like it when you yell at them."

Alucard stared at him, his breath softening. The irritation ebbed, pulled away by Zalith's touch. "I like vhen *you* yell at people," he murmured back, reaching up to touch the side of Zalith's neck in turn, his fingers curling gently against his skin.

Zalith leaned in until their foreheads touched. His smile lingered, softer now. "We make a pretty good couple, don't we?" Then, he kissed him once, twice, and again, letting it linger.

Alucard had no objections. He wanted this just as much as Zalith did—he *needed* it. So he gave in to the demon's slow, coaxing kisses, melting into them with a soft breath and a hand curled in the fabric at Zalith's waist. For a moment, the world outside the alley faded. Nothing mattered but this.

Then Zalith pulled back slightly, his breath warm against Alucard's lips, eyes burning into his. "If I find somewhere for us to hide," he murmured, a smirk ghosting across his mouth, "can you fuck me?"

The question hit like a ripple across calm water, one that cracked straight through the fragile peace Alucard had just started to feel. Hesitation clawed up his spine. He wanted Zalith's affection; he craved it, he *ached* for it. But not like this. Not if it meant disappointment. Not when the shame was already simmering beneath his skin. He hadn't made Zalith climax once. Every time ended with guilt and a drowning feeling of inferiority. Why would this time be any different?

He opened his mouth to speak, to explain and back out gently, but before he could, Zalith smiled again.

"Or…" Zalith offered eagerly, "I can fuck you."

The hesitation didn't vanish. It never did. Any kind of intimacy lately made something in him twist, and he couldn't shake it. He wanted to want it, but the weight of his own discomfort always crept in too soon.

"Ve 'ave vings to do," he mumbled, his voice low, avoiding Zalith's gaze. "And I'm tired vight now. But…maybe later vhen ve get 'ome." Even as he said it, he knew it wasn't true. He'd felt this way for weeks now, and it wasn't fading. If anything, it was settling deeper, and no matter how much he loved Zalith, no matter how much he wanted to give him everything, no matter how much he wanted to dismiss the truth of what he was, this was the one part of himself he still couldn't seem to control.

"Okay," Zalith said softly, pulling his hand away and stepping back.

Alucard saw the shift instantly—the flicker of disappointment in his eyes, the subtle dip in his voice. It hit him like a knife to the ribs, and guilt twisted through his chest. He hated this. He hated how much he'd turned Zalith down. He knew what it must look like…that he wasn't interested anymore. That he didn't want him. But that wasn't it at all. He *did* want Zalith in *every way*. He treasured every moment they shared whether they were tangled in a kiss or just sitting in silence. Though no matter how badly he craved closeness, this choking sense of inadequacy clung to him like a second skin, and no amount of love seemed to be enough to tear it away.

He watched as Zalith fastened his coat's top button to let the dragonlet wriggle up and get some air. "I'm sorry," he said sullenly, reaching out for Zalith's hand. "I vant to,

I just…I veel so tired vrom today, and ve still 'ave vings to do bevore ve can velax," he said, moving closer as he held his hand tightly.

"It's probably better that we don't because I'm sure she'd have something to say about it," he said, glancing down at the dragonlet. "If it's okay, I think we should find somewhere to let her stretch out for a few minutes before we leave."

Zalith still sounded upset, and Alucard's guilt grew into an almost painful pit in his chest. But what more could he say? He felt far too anxious to admit the truth—maybe he should just tell him. He hated keeping things from Zalith…but he felt so humiliated about it—so…stupid, even, to let something like this ruin their intimacy, especially since Zalith had told him that none of it bothered him, that the truth of his gender wasn't a problem.

Still, he didn't know what to do. He didn't know why he was like this, why he took so long to say what he needed to say.

Would Zalith be angry with him? No…well…he didn't know what to think. All he knew was that the thought of telling Zalith made him feel nauseatingly embarrassed.

He let it go. He'd tell him another time.

With a nod, he said, "Ve can take 'er outside zhe city."

"Okay. Thank you."

Zalith then led the way out of the alley.

Snow started falling, layering over the drizzle that had clung to the city earlier. It dusted the rooftops, caught in the glow of the streetlamps, and whispered across the cobblestones like ash. Alucard didn't really notice the cold anymore; guilt had already sunk its claws in too deep.

As they walked through the moonlit streets towards the city's edge, silence stretched between them. It wasn't comfortable. It wasn't earned. It felt like a bruise.

He kept his eyes low, watching the fresh snow settle over their path, and tried not to crumble beneath the weight in his chest. He'd upset Zalith *again*. The guilt gnawed at him mercilessly. He wished he could just *shut off* the feelings of inadequacy that haunted him. But they clung like barbed hooks, buried too deep to pull out. Every time he turned Zalith down, they tugged tighter and tore deeper. He *hated* saying no; he *hated* the way Zalith's smile dimmed each time, even when he tried to hide it.

And it wasn't because he didn't want him. The need for that intimacy never left him. But his thoughts were a snare, dragging him under before he could even reach for it. What if Zalith could tell? What if he *knew* that sometimes, he felt so *numb* that he couldn't enjoy it at all? That sometimes he felt so foreign in his own skin that he didn't want to be *seen*?

He lifted a gloved hand and brushed his fingers lightly along his jawline—delicate, almost too much so for a man. His features had changed since the discovery. Subtle. Feminine. Wrong. And in his reflection, he didn't know who he was looking at anymore.

He swallowed hard and tried to breathe past the ache in his throat. He couldn't fight off the thought. He wasn't a real man. Not fully. Not really. And what did that make him? What kind of partner couldn't even *satisfy* the man he loved? What kind of demon *denied* his mate the connection he so clearly needed?

Zalith was an incubus. This wasn't just about pleasure, it was about energy and *bonding*, and Alucard was starting to deny him that.

His shame deepened as he stole a glance at the demon beside him, silent, unreadable. He knew Zalith wouldn't push. He never did. But that only made it worse.

There *was* something he could do, a compromise he'd made before when his own mind betrayed him. He'd wait until they got home, where it was safer, where he could take care of Zalith in other ways…even if he couldn't let him in—not all the way.

"I don't want to bring the dragon anywhere potentially dangerous," Zalith said at last, breaking the silence. "You've already flown us so far today, and I don't think it's a good idea for you to fly us all the way home, drop her off, and then fly all the way back out here again for Opus' stupid list. We should call it a night. I'll send him a message."

Alucard kept his gaze fixed on the snow-glazed street, his shoulders slightly hunched beneath his cape. The frost in his throat made his answer quieter than intended. "Okay."

Zalith glanced at him. "Unless you'd rather we get it over with. But if you're tired, I think you should rest."

He nodded, still not looking up. "Ve can vest. Ve'll 'ead out in zhe morning."

There was no argument from Zalith this time, just a silent agreement between them—unspoken but understood.

They walked on, their boots muffled by the snow. The city stretched around them in shades of silver and shadow, tall buildings with dragon-headed gables looming overhead.

Alucard stole one last glance at Zalith, who was holding the baby dragon close inside his coat, his expression unreadable beneath the falling snow. He ached to reach for his hand, to say *something*…but the words refused to come.

So instead, they walked in silence through the frost-bitten city—together, but not quite close enough.

| **Zalith** |

| *Avalmoor, Drakalyth Region, Crytharion City Outskirts* |

The further away from the city they walked, the harder it got for Zalith to keep a frown off his face. He didn't understand why Alucard didn't want to have sex. Was something wrong? Was it him? No... Alucard said he was tired... but this wasn't the first time he'd said that, and normally, he didn't say no to him, so... maybe it *was* him.

Was Alucard not attracted to him anymore?

Was he tiring of him?

He didn't know what to think, and as much as he wanted answers, he was afraid to ask in case Alucard said something he didn't want to hear.

He tried to dismiss his thoughts, following Alucard off the main path. If things didn't improve soon, he'd *have* to say something. There was obviously a reason why Alucard was saying no, and whatever it was, he'd find out sooner or later.

"Ve can probably let 'er out 'ere vor a moment," Alucard said as he led Zalith behind a large dead oak tree.

Zalith came to a halt, casting a quick glance over his shoulder at the city in the far distance and then ahead at the length of empty tundra. Snowflakes drifted lazily in the moonlight, and aside from the occasional glow from the bird-sized glow bugs, the world was still and quiet. No one in sight. Good.

Satisfied, he undid his coat buttons and gently reached inside. The dragonlet pressed against his chest gave one last sleepy flutter before he drew her out. Crouching low, he let her slip from his arms and into the snow.

She landed softly, chirping with a faint trill as she rose onto her hind legs, her wings unfurling like delicate fans. For a moment, she was motionless, nose twitching, pupils wide. She lowered herself and sniffed the snow, her movements cautious and feline.

Then, confidence bloomed.

She leapt forward and pounced once, twice, sending up a fine mist of powder as she pranced and dove through it like a hunting fox. Her joy was immediate and infectious, and Zalith found himself smiling. She'd never seen snow before, and in that moment, watching her play so freely, he was glad he'd let her.

"Are you annoyed vith me?" Alucard suddenly mumbled.

Zalith frowned and looked at him. "For what?"

"Vor not vanting to 'ave sex."

"If you don't want to, you don't want to, Alucard. It shouldn't matter whether or not I'm annoyed."

The vampire shrugged, watching the dragonlet as she scurried through the snow.

Zalith didn't know what else to say. He didn't want to tell him that he *was* annoyed because he didn't want Alucard to agree to have sex simply because he didn't want him to be upset. As much as Alucard's disinterest hurt him, he didn't want him to do something he didn't want to do.

"Did you vink about calling 'er Morgana?" Alucard asked quietly.

"Not really," the demon said, a little grateful for the subject change... though the disappointment lingered.

Alucard shrugged. "She veally likes zhe snow. You could call 'er Snowvlake," he said with a smirk. "Or… Vlykra—means snowvlake in Drydenish."

"Maybe. We should start writing these down, but I'm definitely not naming her Snowflake."

The vampire laughed amusedly. "I vink is a cute name."

"For a Pomeranian."

Alucard smiled. "Someving vill come to you. Anyvay…should ve 'ead back now? Bevore gets dark."

"It doesn't matter if something comes to me, because I want *you* to be the one who comes up with the idea so I can approve it," the demon said firmly. "But yes, we can head back now." He picked the dragonlet up.

The vampire sighed a little. "I vill keep vinking," he said, and then he took hold of Zalith's hand once he'd secured the dragonlet in his coat. "Are you veady?"

Zalith nodded.

Alucard wrapped his arms around him, dematerialized them both, and hurried into the sky, heading home.

| **Alucard** |
| *Aestrael, Uzlia Isles, Usrul, Castle Reiner* |

It took two hours to return to Uzlia—longer than usual, and far more draining.

When Alucard rematerialized in the castle courtyard, a wave of vertigo crashed into him so violently that it made it almost impossible to breathe. He staggered back with a quiet snarl, his hand slapping against the stable wall to keep himself upright. The cold stone pressed into his palm, making him shiver.

He closed his eyes, waiting for the nausea to pass.

It didn't.

The ground beneath his boots felt unstable, like it was dissolving, and a high-pitched ringing filled his skull, shrill and unbearable. His stomach churned, and for a split second, he feared he might collapse right.

A hand touched his shoulder.

He flinched, grimaced, and forced his eyes open—only to find Zalith standing in front of him. The demon's mouth was moving, but his voice reached him as nothing more than a warped hum…it sounded as though it was echoing from behind a wall of glass.

"…okay?" Zalith asked. "Alucard?"

Staring at him, Alucard frowned, stepping back so that he could lean his back against the wall. The dizziness…the *weakness*…it was unlike anything he'd felt before. It was almost like what he'd experienced years ago when transporting vampires through the portal had become too much for him.

"Let me help you inside," Zalith said, his voice twisting through the distortion.

Alucard couldn't find his voice, but he gave a small, shaky nod. His body ached, and when Zalith slipped an arm around his back and guided his own across his shoulders, a sharp jolt of pain pulsed through his side, pulling a strained grunt from his throat.

He clenched his jaw but didn't pull away.

Zalith tightened his grip and began leading him across the damp stone towards the castle's front doors.

And then everything became a blur.

He saw a glimpse of the entrance hall.

Another of the lounge.

And then he felt the soft couch beneath him.

"Alucard?" Zalith asked worriedly.

Alucard felt the demon's warm palm against his cheek. He set his eyes on Zalith, staring…almost as if he didn't understand who he was for a moment.

Of course he knew who he was.

So why did he feel…confused?

"Do you want blood?" Zalith asked.

Alucard kept staring for a moment, the demon's words echoing through his head. He knew what he wanted to say, it just seemed to take a little longer than usual for him to work out *how* to say it.

And then he nodded. "Yes," he murmured finally. "Please."

Zalith unbuttoned his coat, letting the dragonlet out.

As she pounced out onto the couch beside the demon, she scurried along it and hid herself under one of the cushions, watching Zalith, waiting with a playful look on her face.

The demon quickly pulled off his coat and blazer, and then he moved his hand to the back of Alucard's head and guided his face closer to his neck.

Alucard didn't hesitate. His hand found Zalith's shoulder, gripping it tight, and with a quiet exhale, he leaned in and sank his fangs into the warm curve of the demon's neck.

Zalith flinched before a soft, breathy sigh left his lips, pleasure curling at the edges.

The moment Alucard began to swallow, the pain started fading. Strength threaded its way back into his limbs, slow but steady, chasing off the numbness like sunlight breaking through fog. He hummed low against Zalith's throat, eyes fluttering shut as the heat settled inside him. Zalith's fingers brushed gently through his hair, and a shiver rolled through him, not the cold kind but the kind that was almost pleasing and tender.

Still, he didn't want to take more than he needed.

After a few mouthfuls, he slowed. Then, with a small, reluctant frown, he drew his fangs from Zalith's neck. He dragged his tongue across the punctures, sealing them before letting his head rest against Zalith's shoulder. He nuzzled softly into the other side of his neck, and Zalith's chin came to rest atop his head.

Warm. Close. Safe. *Relief.*

"Vank you," he murmured as the demon's blood granted him a comforting high. "I zon't know…I zon't know vhy I velt so…exhausted."

"You've been flying us all around the world today," Zalith said quietly. "Maybe you just need to rest."

He frowned, staring at what he could see of Zalith's neck. There was something he wanted to do…something he told himself he was going to do once they got home. But what was it? He attempted to think, but his head was so fuzzy—so…*confused.* "No," he mumbled. "I vanted…zhere vas someving I vanted to do," he said, pouting.

"What did you want to do?"

Alucard *demanded* that the thought return. He recalled that what he wanted to do was for Zalith, but…what? His high was making it hard to think—hard to remember. He stroked his hand down his mate's body…and when he remembered, a smile made its way onto his face. "I vanted…I vant to suck your dick."

Zalith laughed slightly. "Why?"

The vampire pouted again. "Because I vant to."

"Thank you for the offer, but I want you to rest."

Alucard frowned. He wasn't expecting him to say no. "You zon't…vant me to?"

"Of course I want you to, but your well-being is more important to me right now."

He sighed a deep, long sigh and let his head sink to Zalith's chest. "Okay," he mumbled. "I vill vest…vight…'ere," he muttered, letting himself relax entirely, closing his eyes. "You can vest vith me."

The demon laughed quietly as he leaned back and made himself comfortable. "Okay."

As Alucard let himself slowly drift off to sleep, though, the pain started creeping back in. He did his best to ignore it, though. All he needed was some rest…*actual rest*…and then he'd be fine.

Chapter Fourteen

— ⸱ † ⸱ —

Bath

| **Alucard—***Sunday, Aprilis 16th, 960(TG)* |
| *Uzlia Isles, Usrul, Castle Reiner* |

Alucard stirred with a faint frown, waking slowly from what was meant to be a nap…though judging by the stiffness in his limbs, it had been far longer. As his eyes blinked open, he found himself staring up at the rib-vaulted ceiling of his and Zalith's bedroom. The chandelier hung motionless above, its gold arms empty of light.

Zalith must have carried him upstairs after they got home last night.

Birdsong filtered through the tall windows, soft and distant, accompanied by a faint ringing in his ears that hadn't yet faded. Sunlight streaked across the pale stone walls in long, angled rays; the curtains had been left open, likely by Zalith. Though the light didn't bother him like it usually would. It felt…oddly grounding.

He hadn't dreamt this time. No memories had come to him. But he wasn't sure whether that was a good thing or not. No more answers, but…no overbearing emotions the second he woke up.

The next thing he noticed was the weight against his right side. He turned his head and found Zalith there, asleep, head resting on his shoulder, one arm draped securely across his torso. The demon held him like something precious, as if even in sleep he wasn't willing to let go.

Alucard exhaled softly, the tension in his body loosening as a quiet smile curved his lips. He tilted his head just slightly, enough to rest it gently against Zalith's, and closed his eyes again, content to linger in the stillness.

A few moments later, Zalith began to stir. His body shifted gently against Alucard's as he woke, and a quiet nuzzle to the vampire's neck was followed by a languid stretch. "Good morning, darling," he mumbled sleepily, his lips brushing the side of Alucard's throat before pressing a kiss there.

Alucard smiled and kissed the top of Zalith's head in return. "Good morning, my love."

Zalith eased himself forward, his body settling slowly atop Alucard's, chest to chest, arms braced on either side. He gazed down at him with a quiet sort of joy, his eyes soft; he brushed the loose strands of hair from Alucard's face, and then he leaned in to kiss him.

Their lips met, and when Zalith pulled back, Alucard felt the last threads of last night's pain dissolve into the sunlight.

"Hi," the vampire murmured, his voice barely above a breath as he looked up at him, smiling.

"Hi," Zalith said softly, caressing his hair. "Do you feel any better?"

He nodded slightly. "I veel a lot better, vank you."

"Good," he said and kissed his lips again.

An impulsive flicker of playfulness stirred in Alucard's chest, a rare shift from the heaviness that usually followed him. Without thinking twice, he gripped Zalith's left shoulder and gave him a gentle shove, rolling him onto his back and sliding over him. Now above him, Alucard smiled down at the demon, a faint spark in his eyes. He leaned in, his hair falling forward slightly, and pressed a slow kiss to Zalith's lips…then another, and one more for good measure, each one softer than the last but full of affection.

For a moment, Zalith looked hopeful, and Alucard knew why.

But he didn't overthink it.

He kept kissing him, letting himself sink into the warmth of Zalith's lips. A quiet shiver coursed through him as the demon's hand slid up to caress the side of his neck, fingers brushing just beneath his jaw. Every kiss deepened the pull between them, teasing sparks of desire across his skin. That familiar ache stirred low inside him, rising with every press of Zalith's mouth. His instincts were quickly set alight, woken from the sleep he'd buried them into. This time, though, he didn't deny what his heat-enthralled body longed for.

His hand trailed lower, fingertips grazing the demon's chest, then down his torso. He wanted this. He wanted Zalith. He could feel the hunger building in him, the ache to be close, to feel *claimed*. But just as the words *fuck me* began to form in his mind, a flicker of hesitation pierced through.

Those same old thoughts came creeping back. What if he couldn't give Zalith what he needed? What if he wasn't enough?

He didn't want to let the fear win.

He remembered what he'd said last night, what he'd promised himself. Zalith deserved his trust, his effort…and his vulnerability, and Alucard *wanted* to give that to him.

So, swallowing the thorns of doubt, he leaned in for another kiss, and as it lingered, he slid his hand down to Zalith's crotch and closed his fingers around the demon's arousal, the touch a quiet answer to the hope in his mate's eyes.

Zalith smiled against his lips, his breath warm and eager as their kisses deepened. His hands slid over Alucard's sides with a slow, reverent pressure before settling on his ass, giving it a firm, greedy squeeze. The vampire laughed and tilted his head to begin kissing down Zalith's neck.

He moved gradually, letting his mouth explore the demon's skin, teasing him. Each kiss was a promise, each flick of his tongue a gentle claim. Zalith sighed beneath him, fingers gliding along Alucard's back before curling in his hair as the vampire trailed lower and beneath the blanket.

Alucard paused at Zalith's waist. He nipped him there, just enough to earn a quiet, breathy laugh, and he grinned against his skin as Zalith's hand gripped his hair a little tighter. Then, with a look upward and a subtle shift of his shoulders, Alucard continued his descent, pressing kisses further down until he reached the heat between Zalith's legs, where all teasing ended.

Alucard took his time, dragging his tongue up the length of Zalith's hardening dick. He stroked his shaft with his hand while he gently sucked and licked the tip, swirling his tongue around it as the demon groaned pleasurably. Once he tasted the sweet warmth of pre-cum, he eased Zalith's dick into his mouth, letting his lips glide over each inch.

The demon's soft, pleased hum sent a flicker of pride through him, easing some of the tension that still lingered in his chest. The taste, the warmth, the way Zalith's body responded beneath him—it relieved him, it *soothed* him. As his tongue traced slowly along the hard, thick length, he felt Zalith's thighs shift, and another quiet, satisfied moan escaped his mate.

The sound of it only encouraged him.

Alucard adjusted his position, moving with slow confidence, letting himself enjoy the weight of Zalith's arousal against his tongue. He felt Zalith's fingers slide into his hair, cradling the back of his head with a firm yet tender grip. The vampire shivered again, part from arousal, part from the intimacy.

When the bedcovers rustled and shifted, Alucard glanced up from beneath his lashes. Zalith had pushed the blankets aside to look down at him properly, his dark eyes heavy with desire, his hand still buried in Alucard's hair as if he couldn't bear to let him go.

Alucard kept his pace unhurried, letting his mouth and tongue work Zalith towards the edge. Every low, breathless sound the demon made vibrated through him, each one stoking a mix of satisfaction and longing. He could feel the tension building in Zalith's body, the way his fingers tightened in his hair, the faint arch of his hips, the quiet growl curling in his throat.

The vampire pressed closer, deepening his rhythm just enough to draw a sharp moan from above. Zalith's breaths grew heavier, his grip almost possessive now, and Alucard knew he was close. That knowledge sparked a faint thrill in him; he liked knowing he could bring him to this point, even if the ache of his own self-doubt lingered like a shadow.

When Zalith finally let go, his climax came with a delighted, relieved whine that filled the room. Alucard eased him through it, slowing, softening as he swallowed every drop. Only once the demon's hold loosened did he kiss his way back up his body, tasting the faint sweetness of skin warmed by pleasure.

At his neck, Alucard lingered, nuzzling into him while catching his breath, feeling the steady rise and fall of Zalith's chest as he calmed. He wished the moment filled him with the same contentment it seemed to give his mate; he was glad to have pleased him—he always was—but the weight of his recent thoughts still clung to him, stubborn and cold. He'd just have to push it down.

He moved his face from Zalith's neck and smiled down at him.

The demon's hand came up to stroke Alucard's cheek, his touch warm and almost coaxing. "Do you want a turn?" he asked with a smirk.

Alucard nodded without hesitation—but the moment he did, something twisted inside him. He *wanted* this…at least part of him did. The other part—the part that whispered doubts and fed his anxiety—stirred almost immediately. The more he thought about it, the heavier it pressed against him.

He forced himself not to dwell on it.

Zalith eased him onto his back and leaned down to claim his lips. Alucard let himself sink into the kiss, bringing a hand up to the back of the demon's head, fingers threading into the silken strands. His mate's scent, his warmth, the faint weight of him above—all of it was almost enough to drown out the tension clawing at his thoughts.

Then Zalith's hand slid lower, curling around his arousal in a slow, teasing caress, and Alucard's breath caught against his mouth. He kissed him back, harder this time, holding onto the moment as though he could keep the doubts from creeping in.

When Zalith began kissing his way down his body, Alucard let his head sink back into the pillows, eyes falling shut. Each press of the demon's lips left a trail of warmth that lingered against his skin, easing the tension from his muscles. He exhaled slowly, willing himself to relax, to be present.

The first sweep of Zalith's tongue over his dick pulled a quiet hum from his throat, pleasure curling through him in a slow, creeping tide. The demon's heat and the wet glide of his mouth were enough to loosen the last of his restraint. Alucard slipped his hands beneath the cover, fingers tangling in Zalith's hair, holding on as though anchoring himself there.

When Zalith truly began to please him, working him with a steady, unhurried rhythm, something heady and deeply satisfying took root in his chest. He obediently spread his legs as Zalith gave his thighs a gentle push, and the moment the demon eased his dick into his throat, Alucard let out a delighted whine, and the rest of the world fell away. Here, there was only the warmth, the touch, and the steady pulse of pleasure.

It didn't take long for him to reach the edge; too long without this had left him far too ready; and when he came, his intense orgasm left him trembling in the aftershocks, his breath shallow, his heart racing. His body felt satisfied, and his instincts stopped clawing at him…only for a few fleeting seconds, though.

His heat demanded more.

Zalith slowly kissed his way back up the vampire's body, each press of his lips a lingering spark in the wake of pleasure.

Alucard's smile was content as his hand found the side of the demon's neck, thumb brushing over the warm skin there. Their mouths met in a slow, lingering kiss…and a few short kisses followed before Zalith let out a quiet sigh against his lips. The demon's fingers drifted into his hair, idly toying with the crimson strands, as though reluctant to let the moment end.

"I should probably get up and feed the dragon," Zalith suddenly said.

Alucard frowned. *The dragon.* How could he have forgotten? "Vhere did you put 'er?"

The demon glanced over at the chest of drawers over by the far-left wall. The middle drawer was open with a bundle of blankets inside. *That* was obviously where he'd put her.

"Do you vant my 'elp?" he offered.

The demon smiled as he stroked the side of Alucard's face. "No, thank you. But maybe you could run us a bath," he suggested.

He nodded. "Okay. Should I meet you in zhere? Zhe bavroom."

Zalith nodded. "We might be a bit, though. I have to tell Edwin to bring her food up here."

Alucard shrugged. "Is okay. Vill take a vhile to vill zhe bath anyvay."

"Let me know when it's done," the demon said. He kissed Alucard's lips, got out of bed, and went over to the drawer.

Alucard stepped into the bathroom and turned the taps, letting the steady rush of water fill the quiet. Steam began to curl into the cool air as he reached for his robe, pulling it around himself before settling on the edge of the bath.

He watched the water rise, the surface rippling under the flow, and then he reached for the bottle and let a ribbon of bubble bath slip into the stream. The scent lifted into the air almost instantly, but his focus had already drifted back to the lingering weight of earlier. The satisfaction he'd hoped for hadn't come, not fully. He doubted Zalith had felt entirely fulfilled either, and a faint sting of guilt pressed in at the thought. No matter how he tried to shove the anxiety aside, it clung, keeping him from crossing that final line with Zalith. It was maddening, wanting him, needing that closeness, but feeling his own mind bar the way.

Alucard let out a slow breath, eyes fixed on the water curling higher in the tub. Why couldn't he just push past it? Why couldn't he move on and stop letting it gnaw at him? Deep down, he already knew.

The humiliation. *So much of it.*

He already felt like less of a man standing beside him, and less of a demon, too. Disavowed. An outcast. To most of their kind, he was worth no more than a sneer, and usually, he could take it, but when that scorn was aimed at him in front of Zalith, it landed differently, cutting deep, making him feel small and forgettable. And this… this inability to give Zalith the same pleasure he received was just another failing to add to the pile.

The weight of it pressed on him like a cold, relentless downpour. He caught his reflection in the faint ripple of the water, jaw tightening, shame and disappointment clawing at him. With another sigh—this one heavier—he shut off the taps, the tub full and waiting, though the heaviness in his chest refused to ease.

Not too long later, Zalith came into the bathroom with the dragonlet following.

Alucard frowned. Had he really been sitting in here *that* long?

"Hey," the demon said with a smile, closing the door behind him as he threw a small cat toy onto the floor, which the dragonlet immediately began to stalk.

He smiled at him, too. "Did you veed 'er?"

"Yeah," he said, making his way over to him. "Is the water still warm?"

The vampire nodded. "Vinished villing up not too long ago."

Zalith climbed into the water, and as he did, Alucard pulled off his bathrobe and joined him.

"Did you tell Opus zhat ve'd be getting vhat 'e vanted today instead?" the vampire asked.

"I did," he confirmed as he made Alucard turn and lean his back against his chest.

As he made himself comfortable, he sighed. "Vhen should ve leave? Zhe best place to vind arachnoids and snow viends is Avalmoor—zhe more norvhern parts."

"We should have breakfast first, and then I need to talk to Edwin about watching her while we're gone," he said, nodding down at the dragonlet as she chased the small cat toy around the bathroom floor.

Alucard nodded. "Vhen ve get 'ome, I vill probably start making you zhat 'olster," he said, taking hold of the hand Zalith had rested on his chest. "I vill vork on getting you your own colts, too."

"Thank you," Zalith said contently. "Why does Opus want us to get these things for him if they're so close to where he lives?"

"Vell…is dangerous, and 'e probably zoesn't vant to visk 'urting 'imselv…or dying," he mumbled. "Arachnoids are 'ard to take down, especially zhe queens. And zhen snow viends are vormidable. Zhey are veally 'ard to detect and vone 'it could break every bone in a man's body—luckily, ve are not ordinary men," he explained with a small smirk.

"What even is a snow fiend?"

"Is a…big…volf-like monster. About eight veet tall…scary vace…very loud voar, big talons," he said, holding out his own claws. "As vhite as zhe snow."

"Oh. I was thinking we were up against a yeti or something," the demon laughed.

"Yeti?"

"It's a…giant…monkey person—they like living in the cold."

Alucard frowned. "Oh…vell…no. A snow viend is more like verevolf if anyving."

"Makes sense," the demon said. "As far as I'm aware, yetis are fairly peaceful unless disrespected."

"Vell, maybe ve can get zhis egg vithout even 'aving to vace zhe viend. Zhey leave zheir nests to vind vood vairly ovten."

"Ew…wait, they're like wolves, but they lay eggs?"

The vampire nodded. "Zhey are big, vurry lizards zhat look like verevolves."

"That makes more sense."

"And zhen an arachnoid is just big spider."

"Which one is worse?"

"Spiders," Alucard grumbled. "Ve 'ave to go to a nest to vind a queen, so zhere vill be vhousands of zhem."

"Are you sure we can handle it alone?" the demon asked, sounding conflicted.

"Ve 'ave vire," Alucard said with a nod. "Ve vill be vine."

"That's true," Zalith said as he lightly stroked his fingers along Alucard's chest. "When I was younger, my cousins used to light ants on fire with my uncle's monocle, which he wore strictly for what he referred to as fashion," he said amusedly. "My dad used to wear one sometimes, too."

Alucard laughed a little. "Veally?"

"Yeah," Zalith laughed with him. "Both parts."

The vampire turned around so that he was facing Zalith and rested his body against his. "Maybe ve can get a big enough monocle to burn all zhe spiders avay, no?"

"Only if you carry it."

Alucard smiled, closing his eyes as he relaxed. "I zon't vink vould be practical—maybe ve should stick to zhe vire ve crveate vith our own 'ands and save zhe monocle vor if ve ever 'ave to vace giant ants."

"I hope that's a day that never comes," Zalith mumbled, moving his arms around him.

Alucard smiled. "Me too."

Chapter Fifteen

— ⸱ ✝ ⸱ —

Arachnoids

| Alucard |
| *Avalmoor, Solcrathis Region, Wraithpine Hollow* |

After breakfast—and after a two-hour flight—Alucard descended into the heart of a dead forest, rematerializing with Zalith. The world here exhaled frost with every breath of wind. They stood among blackened trunks, the skeletal remains of trees that clawed at the pewter sky as if still begging for life. Snow crusted the ground in brittle patches, but the earth beneath it was a strange ashen grey, the colour of something long burned to nothing.

Avalmoor hadn't changed. The air carried a metallic tang, like old blood and charred bone, and the silence pressed in heavily, broken only by the occasional groan of a tree swaying, though there was no wind strong enough to move it. Wisps of cold mist curled between the trunks, drifting low to the ground, almost as if the forest itself still breathed in its sleep.

"Zhis is Vraivhpine 'ollow," the vampire said, looking around. "Zhe 'umans near zhis place tell stories about 'ow zhe ashes of Solcravhis are scattered 'ere, zhat zhey curse every living ving zhat tries to grow."

"Spooky," Zalith murmured.

Alucard smiled, taking hold of the demon's hand. "Is not zhat bad," he said as he began leading the way forward. "Zhis is zhe kind of place ve should expect to vind arachnoids."

"Why do they like it here?"

He shrugged. "Zhey are very territorial and protective; zhey live in places most ozzer vings vouldn't be able to so zhat zhey can mass-produce in peace—sort of like zemon matriarchs." He paused and smirked amusedly. "Zidn't Ysmay live out 'ere a vew years ago?"

Zalith shook his head. "I don't want to think about her right now. But yes."

Alucard lost his smile. Mentioning Ysmay probably made Zalith think about Varana. He didn't want him to be upset, so he shifted his focus back to the task. "Ve're probably going to 'ave to go into a cave," he told him, trying to fight the now rising anxiety that came with the idea of walking into a dark, narrow passage… again. Just like the tunnels and catacombs in Atheson, a spider den was going to remind him of where he'd grown up. But he did his best to keep hold of his composure.

"I really hate getting dirty," the demon said with a sigh. "I probably should've prepared myself mentally beforehand—I should've brought those boots we had made."

The vampire shrugged… but then grimaced. "Vill be vebs in zhere. Lots… and lots of vebs."

"Ew," Zalith grumbled.

"You can vait outside if you like," he offered with a smirk.

"Maybe I will," he replied with a teasing smirk of his own.

Alucard smiled again. "Von't be *zhat* bad, zon't vorry. Just zon't touch anyving."

"I'll try and keep my wandering hands to myself."

Alucard's gaze then fixed on what could only be the entrance to the arachnoid nest. Up ahead yawned a cavernous maw in the earth, its stone lip draped in a curtain of thick, tangled webs. The silken strands swayed faintly in the cold air, clinging together in twisting ropes and veils that glistened faintly under what little light reached them. Some hung low like snare lines, others stretched taut across the opening as though spun with malice.

Beyond the pale, shrouded threshold lay nothing but a blackness so deep that it seemed to swallow the light whole. The cold draft that crept out from it smelled faintly of damp stone and musk, almost sweet… predatory.

They stopped at the threshold, the silence between them edged with the same reluctant tension. Even without stepping inside, Alucard could sense the weight of the things that dwelled here… and the dozens of smaller shapes that might be watching from just out of sight.

"Vell… looks like zhat's vhere ve 'ave to go," the vampire said, glancing at Zalith, his heart starting to race in his chest—he wanted to back away… but he knew he couldn't.

His mate looked disgusted, staring into the web-covered cave. "Okay," he uttered.

"Are you sure you vant to go in?"

"Yeah. I'm not going to let you go alone—you can't get rid of me that easily, Alucard," he said playfully, squeezing the vampire's hand.

"I'm glad you're coming vith me. I probably vouldn't go in zhere alone anyvay," he mumbled. Then, as the sound of water dripping inside the cavern grew louder, he frowned hesitantly and looked at Zalith. "Do you vant to lead zhe vay?"

"No," he answered immediately.

Alucard exhaled slowly, trying to push the edge of fear from his mind. "Okay…let's go," he murmured, squeezing Zalith's hand a little tighter before stepping towards the gaping, web-draped maw.

Zalith stayed close, his presence steady beside him. Out of the corner of his eye, Alucard caught the way the demon's gaze flicked over the walls, his coat, and even the ground as though calculating every step to keep the clinging threads and damp slush from brushing against him. It was almost enough to distract Alucard from the oppressive air that seemed to thicken the deeper they went.

Almost.

The narrow passage widened, swallowing them into a vast chamber. Webs stretched in grotesque arcs overhead, thick as rope in some places, so dense that they blotted out what little light their eyes had adjusted to. Shapes hung suspended in the silken mesh— bodies bound tight, their outlines just visible beneath the pale wrapping. Some were the size of men, others no more than hunting dogs. All of them still. All of them *long* dead.

The scent here was worse—stale and sour, like decay wrapped in oily threads.

Alucard's gaze flicked to Zalith once more before sweeping across the cavern, every shadow and strand of web scrutinized. He let his sensory ethos unfurl, searching for the faintest flicker of life, but the chamber felt empty. No heartbeats, no breath, no rustle of chitin against silk. Either this nest had been abandoned long ago, or its inhabitants were lurking deeper inside.

He turned to Zalith, ready to speak—only for a flicker of white to dart past him. Something small, pale, and winged shot straight at his face. Alucard's heart leapt into his throat as a tiny white moth smacked into him, its frantic buzzing like a trapped wasp. He recoiled with a strangled noise, swatting wildly as it ricocheted at him again and again, a deranged little creature on a suicide mission.

Then came the reinforcements. Dozens—no, *hundreds* poured from the shadows, a chaotic blizzard of wings beating in unison. The cavern filled with the dry, papery whisper of their flight, the sound swelling until it was all he could hear.

Zalith moved instantly, sweeping Alucard into the shield of his coat. The vampire buried his face in the demon's chest, clutching fistfuls of fabric as if it might save him from this winged apocalypse. He squeezed his eyes shut, pressing his hands over his ears to muffle the terrible sound. Moths. Hundreds of them. What did they want? To eat him alive? Strip him to the bone? It seemed entirely possible. He stayed hidden, trusting— no, *praying* that Zalith would slaughter every last one of the wretched things before they so much as brushed against him again.

He felt Zalith swatting them away…and once the noise faded, the demon's embrace loosened.

"Are you okay?" his mate asked, laughing.

Alucard didn't immediately let go. He waited a few moments, and when he *did* let go, he looked around, making sure the moths were gone.

Zalith laughed again.

The vampire scowled and pouted. "Is not vunny," he grumbled.

"It was kind of funny," the demon said, smirking.

"No, vasn't," Alucard argued, hastily moving his fingers through his hair to make sure no moths were caught up in it.

"You're lucky they didn't eat the shirt off your back," Zalith laughed, helping him tidy his hair.

"Zhey probably vould 'ave if you veren't 'ere to save me," he muttered, embarrassed.

"You would've been naked and alone," the demon said, finishing with his hair.

Alucard sighed, looking around for any moths that might not have left. "Zhey probably vould 'ave eaten me."

Laughing *again*, his mate moved his hand to the side of Alucard's neck. "Are you ready?"

The vampire nodded, still looking around for moths.

Zalith smiled faintly, lacing their fingers together before leading him towards the yawning passage ahead.

Alucard kept his eyes fixed forward, though the deeper they went, the more the walls began to close in beneath the weight of what clung to them. Human and animal corpses hung swaddled in thick webbing, their shapes distorted, frozen in silent screams. But it wasn't just the dead that lined the stone. Pale-green, oval shells, each over a foot long, sat clustered in groups of three or four, wedged between bodies like grotesque ornaments. Whatever had once crawled within had long since hatched, leaving behind cracked husks and the sickly residue of hardened slime, brittle as ice.

The floor was littered with a chaos of tracks, tiny, spindly imprints by the thousand, etched into the frost. And the further they pressed into the nest, the more the numbers swelled: more eggs, more shrouded corpses, more prints leading into the dark.

Alucard looked around cautiously, focusing on his surroundings rather than his growing anxiety. "Zhe queen should be in zhe centre of zhis nest," he muttered.

Zalith glanced at him and asked, "How big do you think this nest is?"

"Vell…arachnoids live in groups of at least vive 'undred, so zhis cave system probably goes on vor miles."

"We're going to be here for years."

Alucard laughed a little. "If ve stop somevhere, ve can use our ethos to locate 'er. She vill be vherever zhe most energy is. Queens keep a lot of guards avound zhem, and zhere's probably a million eggs avound 'er, too, so zhat's a lot of energy," he explained. "She von't be 'ard to vind."

The disgusted scowl returned to Zalith's face. "This is gross."

With an amused smile, Alucard let go of his hand. "Vould you like me to search vor 'er?"

"Yes, please," the demon mumbled.

Alucard gave a short nod, shutting his eyes as he let the world fade into darkness. His sensory ethos rippled outward, washing through the winding tunnels. The caverns were vast, layered chambers and twisting arteries stretching for miles in every direction. Without this ability, he doubted he or Zalith would ever stumble upon the queen; she could hide down here forever and they'd die wandering.

He pushed deeper, filtering through the echoes—soft flickers of life scattered across the distance. A handful of small signatures pulsed faintly in separate chambers, arachnoids too small to be their quarry. He pressed on, narrowing his focus until—there. A massive cluster flared into his perception, an overwhelming knot of mixed ethos tangled together.

That had to be her.

Alucard opened his eyes, his frown deepening. "Zhere's a cavern below, about vhree 'undred veet a'ead. I vink zhat's vhere she is."

Zalith's gaze lingered on him for a moment. He glanced towards the darkness ahead, the faint crease between his brows betraying his reluctance. "…All right," he said at last before stepping forward to lead the way.

Alucard fell in beside him, his attention flicking warily over the thick webs veiling the stone walls. The air grew steadily warmer with each step, the closeness of it pricking uncomfortably at his skin. Every sound seemed amplified in the dark—distant drips, the groan of shifting stone, and then a sharper noise: the brittle crack of bone.

Rustling, shuffling…the faint click of many legs skittering over rock.

A tremor of ethos brushed against his senses, small, scuttling signatures too near for comfort. He didn't have to warn Zalith; the demon's own wariness was etched plainly across his face.

Alucard's gaze met Zalith's—

But then everything happened so quickly that Alucard had no time to prevent it.

A spider the size of a wolf shot out of the shadows, its chitinous body slamming into them. They hit the frozen ground in a tangle of limbs and a sickening, wet thud, and the air filled with a frenzy of sound—scraping legs, frantic rustling, and the skittering thunder of more shapes pouring from the black.

Alucard twisted his head, instinct clawing at him to reach Zalith. But the demon lay motionless beside him, blood trickling from his temple in a thin, glistening trail.

"Zaliv—"

Before his fingers could reach his mate, the spider lunged again. Its hooked fangs punched into Zalith's leg, and in a blur of snapping limbs and dragging silk, it yanked the unconscious demon into the shadows.

"Zaliv!" he yelled, panicking. He lunged forward, fingers outstretched to catch Zalith's arm—

Pain ripped through his calf like a blade, and he was wrenched backwards, boots scraping against stone as the spider dragging Zalith vanished into a narrow gap in the wall, the demon's limp form swallowed by the dark.

A furious snarl tore from Alucard's throat. He kicked savagely at the spider clamped to his leg until it skittered away, ichor splattering the rock. He bolted for the gap—

Two massive spiders dropped from above, their bodies thudding onto the stone. Chitinous limbs clattered as they surged towards him, blocking his path before hurling themselves at him.

He had to be fast—he had to get to Zalith.

As the spiders jumped at him, he reached into his cape; he yanked his cane free and pulled the blade from within, swiftly slicing both spiders in half before the sword was entirely free. As their severed bodies hit the ground, Alucard swung around and set his eyes on the other two spiders, which screeched and ran at him. He swung his blade and slew the creatures, and without a moment to waste, he turned, sheathed his sword, and hurried to the gap Zalith had been dragged into.

He propelled himself forward, diving feet-first into the crevasse—Zalith was still alive; he could sense his life force through their imprints. But there was no telling what might happen if he didn't hurry after him.

As he slid down the sloping passageway, he lifted his head just enough to see where he was heading. It had to be taking him down to the main part of the nest. But Zalith had been knocked unconscious, and the arachnoid that had taken him was probably already wrapping him up in webs ready for their queen to devour—he wasn't going to let that happen.

The slope spat him out into open air. Alucard hit jagged rock *hard*, his boots skidding before his knees gave in and sent him crashing to the ground with a sharp grunt. Pain flared, but there was no time to feel it. He scrambled upright, ducking low, and darted for the shadow of a mound of brittle bones.

Peering over them, his search for Zalith froze mid-breath.

The queen.

She loomed against the far cavern wall, her monstrous body suspended in a grotesque cradle of webbing. Black-red chitin glistened in the dim light, her swollen abdomen pulsing as it strained to push out one slick, glistening egg after another, each dropping into a silk cocoon that hung beneath her. Every few seconds, another hit the webbed pouch with a wet sound.

A swarm of lesser arachnoids—still the size of wolves—skittered in, their fangs glinting. They seized the fresh eggs in hooked forelimbs, scurrying them away to an obscene mound in the far left corner. The pile writhed faintly, a sick, shifting hill of glistening green shells.

There had to be over a hundred of them. All moving, all working, dragging corpses, hauling eggs, spinning more webs around still-living prey that twitched and whimpered beneath the silken shrouds. The air reeked of damp rot, venom, blood, decay, and something foul that turned his stomach.

Then he saw him.

Just beyond the bone pile, the spider that had dragged Zalith here was crouched low over its prize. Wispy strands hissed from its spinnerets, winding tight around the demon's feet, layer after glistening layer, inching their way up towards his shins. Zalith's head hung limp, hair spilling across his pale face—still unconscious.

A cold, sharp pulse of panic cut through Alucard's chest. If that web reached higher, he knew exactly what would come next. And he wasn't about to let it get that far.

Keeping low, Alucard cloaked himself in the shadows of his demon ethos, vanishing from the spider's senses. He slipped from behind the bone pile, each step soundless over the jagged stone. The spider's spinnerets twitched, oblivious, until his hand clamped down on its head—the vampire drew the blade from his cane and drove it deep into the creature's skull; the metal punched through with a wet crack, and the spider's body went limp before it could even twitch.

Alucard wrenched the blade free, slicing through the sticky, silk-wrapped bindings around Zalith's feet. Freed, the demon's legs slumped heavily to the floor. Sheathing the weapon, Alucard slid his arms under Zalith's and dragged him back behind the mound of bones, shielding him from the skittering shapes that still haunted the cavern.

"Zaliv?" he murmured, tapping the demon's cheek with his fingertips.

No response. Zalith's head wound had closed, but the dried trail of blood stretched from brow to jaw, a dark stain against his skin. If Alucard tried to wake him with ethos, he risked waking him to a concussion, and in that state, his mate wouldn't be able to fight.

Instead, he slipped off his cape and draped it over Zalith, tucking it close. He needed him hidden and protected. Drawing one claw across his palm, he let a few drops of blood fall onto the demon's skin. The rich scent curled in the air before sinking into him, masking his aura and scent, erasing him from the awareness of anything hunting in this nest. Zalith would hate it if he knew that he was using his blood after yesterday, but this was the only way to keep him safe.

That left one task. The blood of the arachnoid queen.

Alucard's gaze swept the cavern, the restless shapes moving beyond the bone pile. He'd have to be fast. Every second he lingered was another second Zalith lay here alone.

The vampire slipped from the shelter of the bone pile, every muscle poised for speed. The instant his boots hit open ground, a spider clinging to the cavern ceiling twisted towards him. Its fangs clicked, and a shrill, chittering screech tore through the air.

Silence followed. Every other spider froze mid-motion. Dozens of glistening eyes turned to him, their bodies still as if the whole nest had drawn a single breath.

Revulsion coiled inside him, but he shoved it down. This place was filth, every inch of it crawling with nightmares, but if he let disgust slow him now, he'd never reach the queen.

The enormous matriarch reared back, her bloated body swaying as she let out a screech so sharp that it rattled through his skull. One jagged foreleg stabbed through the air, aimed squarely at him—a command.

Alucard bolted straight for her. The cavern erupted around him as every spider within sight surged forward, skittering in a frenzy; from the honeycomb of holes in the walls, more poured out—dozens, maybe hundreds—legs scraping rock, fangs clattering like blades in the dark.

He wasn't here to slaughter them all. That would waste time, energy, and blood. No, he needed the queen's blood, and once he had it, he'd take Zalith and get the hell out of this nest.

In a heartbeat, he sheathed his cane in the holster on his belt and pulled a knife out instead; he sliced his wrist, and as his blood left his body, he commanded it, transforming it into black fog, ensnaring the cavern in darkness in a matter of seconds.

And then he disappeared into vermillion smoke.

As he silently hurried towards the queen, he heard the spiders scurrying around in search of him. But they wouldn't find him.

He weaved through the horde, and once he reached the queen, he rematerialized, pulled his sword from his cane, and sliced one of her legs clean off. She shrieked and hissed as green blood spewed from her severed limb—Alucard wasn't going to waste time shutting her up. He grabbed the severed leg, but before he could dematerialize, one of the spiders lunged and grabbed him, forcing him to the ground.

The vampire wrestled with the creature, grabbing the spider's leg before it could sink its fangs into his neck. As it screeched and squirmed, the queen shrieked and slammed a talon down towards him. He gritted his teeth with a snarl, throwing the spider off and scrambling to his feet just in time to avoid the queen's attack.

But those split seconds of struggle had given his position away to the rest of the nest, and every single spider charged towards him.

Alucard sliced the first spider that jumped at him, his blade making easy work of it. He raced to where the queen's severed leg lay, slaying the swarming creatures in his way. And once he reached it, he picked it up, dematerialized once more, and returned to Zalith.

His fog was starting to thin.

He dropped the spider leg and looked back over his shoulder, setting his eyes on the swarm as they searched for him again—and *of course*, ugly, beady little eyes found him as he pulled his cape back on.

It was time to go.

In his left hand, he picked up the spider leg, and in his right, he gripped Zalith's arm and hastily dematerialized. He raced up the slope and out through the crevasse, taking his mate with him as the spiders chased after him.

He sped up despite the sudden fatigue, and as soon as he got out of the cave, he curved and raced into the sky. Once he was high enough, he stopped and looked down, watching as the avalanche of spiders swarmed the dead tree forest in search of him. Evidently, they had no idea where he'd gone, so it was safe for him to head somewhere he could safely wake Zalith up.

Without a moment of delay, he headed in the direction of the closest settlement.

Chapter Sixteen

Lunch

| **Zalith** |
| *Avalmoor, Solcrathis Region, Wyrm's Rest* |

Zalith grimaced and groaned quietly, a sharp pain surging through his head as he woke. He had no idea where he was; whatever he was lying on was softer than a cave floor, and it didn't smell of damp and dead things. Instead, the smell of something sweet lingered in the air. But as the ache worsened, he opened his eyes and placed his hand over his forehead. "What the fuck?" he muttered, the light of the room clawing at his eyes.

"Zon't try to get up," came Alucard's voice.

He turned his head, setting his eyes on his fiancé, who had just left his seat behind the small desk across the room. But that was exactly what he wanted to do—get up. So he tried to sit, but Alucard sat next to him, placed his hand on his chest, and pushed him back down.

"You 'it your 'ead," the vampire said worriedly.

Staring up at him, Zalith took a moment…and everything started coming back to him. The cave, the spiders…. Had he really been knocked out so easily? He tried to sit up again. "Are you okay?" he asked.

Alucard kept him where he was. "I'm okay. But you're not, so stay in bed."

"I'm fine," he complained, trying to get up—

"You're not indestructible, you know," the vampire said with a pout, weighing his hand down on Zalith's chest to keep him in bed. "If you zon't vest now, you're going to veel vorse later."

Zalith sighed deeply and gave in, relaxing. He looked around, remembering why they'd gone to the cave in the first place. "Did you get the blood?"

Alucard nodded. "I did. I vas just vorking on extracting bevore you voke up," he said, glancing over his shoulder at the desk…where the large leg of a spider was resting.

The demon frowned, looking revolted, and shifted his gaze back to Alucard. "I'm sorry for getting knocked out," he mumbled.

"Is okay," he said, smiling at him. "I like getting to take care of you vor a change," he added with a quiet laugh.

Zalith smiled, but he couldn't help but think about how so many stupid things had happened lately. They'd both suffered what he thought were silly little injuries and inconveniences, things that never really occurred. "Do you think…we're cursed?" he asked with an amused chuckle—he was being sarcastic, of course…mostly.

Alucard frowned. "No. Vhy vould ve be cursed?"

He shrugged and said, "So many stupid little things have been happening to us recently that it seems like being cursed is the only thing that makes sense."

"I zon't vink ve're cursed, ve've just…I zon't know, ve spent zhe last vew veeks…staying 'ome and 'aving sex. And I can't vemember zhe last time ve vaced 'uge spiders," he said, smirking a little. "And 'as been two years since ve vaced Boreas— almost vhree. Ve are just…a little out of touch, maybe. But not cursed."

"I feel cursed," he grumbled.

"Vhy?"

Zalith thought about it. Not only had annoying inconveniences been happening, but there was also the fact that Alucard didn't seem to want to have sex with him. He couldn't help but feel like that was a part of it, too. But he didn't want to talk about it—not yet, at least. He wasn't ready to hear Alucard's answer. So, he shrugged and replied, "Because if it's not one thing, it's another."

"Zhat zoesn't mean ve're cursed," Alucard said, frowning.

He didn't want to explain himself. "Where are we?" he asked, changing the subject.

Alucard's frown thickened. "Ve're in uh…small town bordering zhe territory."

The demon nodded in response.

"Are you 'ungry? Ve could get voom service," the vampire suggested, smirking again.

He took the opportunity and smirked back at him. "Or we could service each other," he said—the pain suddenly worsened, forcing him to grimace and press his palm against the centre of his forehead.

Alucard placed his hand on the side of Zalith's neck. "You von't be doing anyving but lying zhere vor zhe next vhile," he said sternly.

He wouldn't refuse. The last thing he wanted was a migraine. "In that case, I could go for a sandwich," he said, resting his hand on his chest.

Alucard smiled. "Vell, you vait 'ere, and I'll go and order us both someving."

Although it hurt his head, Zalith smiled, too. "Okay. Thank you."

The vampire then got up and quietly left the room.

Zalith exhaled deeply—he didn't want to lie there and think about the things he and Alucard weren't doing, though. He focused on his new dragon instead. Was she getting on fine back home with Edwin? He was sure that she was missing him and probably giving the butler a hard time, but they'd be heading home soon; they just had to go and get a fiend egg, and then this little expedition of theirs would be over.

He sighed and relaxed, closing his eyes while he waited for Alucard to get back.

The door eventually opened.

How long had it been? Zalith couldn't quite tell.

Alucard made his way over to him.

"What did you get?" the demon asked, closing his eyes as his fiancé sat beside him.

"Zhey 'ad a club sandvich ving…so I got us both zhat."

"Thank you," he said with an appreciative smile.

"Do you veel any better? I can give you some of my blood if you like," Alucard offered.

He shook his head. "It's okay. You need it more than I do."

But Alucard pouted sadly in response. "You vere zhe vone who got 'urt, not me."

As much as he wanted Alucard's blood, and as much as he wanted an intimate moment with him, he still felt like he shouldn't accept his offer. "I know, but you should save it," he said, looking up at him. "Because at this rate, we're both probably going to get hurt again."

Alucard frowned, moving his hand over the demon's chest. "I'd vather you 'ave so zhat you're 'ealed vor vhatever ve 'ave to deal vith next," he said softly. "And I zon't like knowing you're 'urt."

Zalith gazed at him. He'd be lying if he said that he hadn't wanted Alucard's blood the moment he offered, and he couldn't refuse a second time. "Okay," he agreed.

Alucard helped him sit, steadying him with a careful hand. Once settled, Zalith leaned in, his gaze locking on the pale stretch of neck offered to him. It had been too long since he'd tasted him, long enough that the hunger thrummed deeper than usual, urging him to bite. So he sank his fangs in, and Alucard flinched, a faint shiver running through his body beneath Zalith's hands, and that tiny reaction only deepened the pleasure that unfurled through him.

Fuck, his blood…so sweet…dark and intoxicating—it rushed through his senses like a fire meant for him alone, smoothing the ache in his muscles, silencing the dull throb in his head. It would be so easy to keep going, to take more, but he forced himself to pull back after one final mouthful.

He didn't leave right away. Instead, he lingered close, his breath brushing Alucard's skin as his thumb swept lazily over the twin punctures his fangs had left. The faint heat of the wounds pulsed beneath his touch, and against his will, his mind began to drift towards the things they weren't doing anymore, the touches and moments that used to follow…the things he wanted, if only Alucard would let him in again.

It was in moments like these that he found he struggled most, though. He'd been fighting his urges and trying to ignore Alucard's pheromones, but it was becoming increasingly difficult. His original instincts were bad enough, but with Alucard being in heat and sitting so close to him…he had to try his very best not to throw himself at him. As much as it pained him, he had to ignore it all.

He frowned sadly and sighed as he nuzzled Alucard's neck.

"Vhat's vrong?" Alucard asked, sounding slightly dazed, likely because of the venom now coursing through his veins.

"Nothing. Thank you for the blood," he mumbled.

"Is okay," the vampire murmured.

Zalith then lay back down, trying to relax.

Alucard helped him make himself comfortable again. He gazed down at him before saying, "Ve can leave zhe viend egg until tomorrow if you vant."

"We're already out here, so we might as well make use of that. But thank you."

The vampire nodded. "If ve 'ead out avter lunch, ve should be done dropping zhem off to Opus by dusk, and zhen ve can 'ead 'ome."

"Okay. Are you going to be okay to fly us home?" he asked, still concerned. "You were really tired yesterday; you pretty much passed out on the couch."

"I'll be vine. A lot 'appened yesterday—dragons and vings…." He smiled at him. "No dragons today."

"I sincerely hope not."

A knock suddenly came at the door.

Alucard looked over his shoulder and called, "Vhat?"

The door opened, and a waiter walked in with two plates. He went to the table that the spider leg was sprawled across, but he didn't seem at all bothered by it. The man placed the plates down, bowed humbly, and then turned around and left without a word.

Alucard got up and brought the plates over. "Zhis is yours," he said, handing one to Zalith.

The demon leaned his back against the headboard. "Thank you." But he didn't really have an appetite anymore. All he could think about was whether Alucard was tired of him. Were his feelings changing? Had he done something wrong to upset his fiancé? He had no idea what was going on. What he *did* know, though, was that if he didn't eat, Alucard would suspect something was wrong, and he *still* wasn't ready to have that conversation.

"So, 'ave you vhought about zhe names I suggested vor zhe dragonlet?"

"Not really. Have you?" he asked and took a bite of his sandwich.

"Vell…no. Do you vant more suggestions?"

"Sure, if you have any."

"I can vink of some," the vampire said, eating his own sandwich. "Do you like zhe sandvich?"

Zalith smiled. "I do, thank you. Do you like yours?"

Alucard nodded. "Is actually veally good," he said contently. "I vas vinking," he then said, "maybe…tomorrow, vonce all of zhis vunning avound vor Opus is over, ve could go and do someving togezzer—like…a date." He paused, turning his head to hide that shy little smile. "'As been a vhile since ve vent on vone."

"I'd like that. Where do you want to go?"

Alucard thought to himself for a few moments. "Vell…maybe ve could go to anozzer opera, or somevhere nice vor dinner."

He smiled at him again; he *did* feel a little better. "We'll have to see what shows are playing."

"Okay," the vampire said.

Zalith then focused on eating. He wasn't sure what to expect from a snow fiend, but he certainly hoped that things would go a lot smoother than they had with the arachnoids.

Chapter Seventeen

— ⸲ ✝ ⸱ —

Fiend Egg

| Zalith |
| *Avalmoor, Maeltharok Region, Mourndrak Vale* |

Side by side, Alucard and Zalith trudged through the drifts, the snow swallowing their boots with each step. More flakes drifted lazily from the grey sky, settling atop the already ten-inch blanket that turned the world into a white monotony.

Zalith's jaw tightened, his expression hard with barely veiled vexation. He was tired of the snow. He wanted nothing more than to be back home, somewhere that didn't creak and crunch beneath every step.

But first came this damn errand. They needed a fiend egg for Opus, and until they found one, there was no point thinking about hearth or home. Alucard at least seemed to have some idea of where to search. Zalith kept pace, his gaze sweeping the frozen horizon and the dark tree line beyond, alert for any threat lurking in the snowbound silence. He'd had enough surprises already. The next one that tried to rear its head, he swore, would not live long enough to make him regret it.

He glanced at Alucard and asked, "Where will we find this fiend egg?"

"Zhe best place to vind vemales and zheir nests is near vrozen lakes because zhey like to vish. You're bound to vind a viend at *every* vrozen lake or river in Avalmoor."

"I wonder what Opus is going to do with it," he muttered. Did he even want to know?

"A lot of people use zhem in alchemy…mostly vor medicines. Zhat's vhat Opus does, vight? 'E's a doctor? Or someving," the vampire mumbled. "Zhese eggs are also probably avound vhree veet tall—snow viends are very big."

"Thank goodness we're strong, I suppose."

Alucard nodded. "Vhen ve vind, ve can store in zhe vault. I'm not carrying zhe ving."

Amused, Zalith laughed quietly. "Okay."

They pressed on through the snow, their path leading towards a vast frozen lake gleaming pale beneath the wan light. No tracks marked the surface, no bird called overhead, and even the wind had stilled, leaving only the steady crunch of their boots breaking the unnatural quiet.

Zalith's shoulders stiffened. The longer they walked, the sharper the feeling gnawed at him, as if a thousand unseen eyes clung to his back, watching and waiting. The silence didn't feel empty at all. It felt hunted.

"I don't like this," the demon mumbled, scanning their surroundings cautiously.

Alucard smiled at him. "Zhe viend is probably vatching us vight now," he said, but he didn't sound anxious. "She von't attack, zhough. She's probably trying to vork out vhether or not ve are a vhreat. Zhe moment she vorks out ve're looking vor zhe nest, zhough, she vill come vor us."

Zalith sighed a tired, deep sigh. "Great. Are they pack creatures?"

"No. Zhey are solitary."

"Good."

When they reached the edge of the lake, they stopped.

The frozen surface looked like it spread for *at least* a mile. It was a lot of terrain to cover, and it was definitely going to take much longer than Zalith wanted.

"Zhey usually keep zheir nests in caves or ditches, vhich zhey vill vith vish and vhatever else zhey kill," Alucard explained. "If zhere *is* an egg 'ere, vill be in zhe same place as zhe vood; viends like to keep everyving…close. Ve vill vind much quicker if ve split up, so you go levt, and I vill go vight."

Zalith didn't like that idea *at all*. "Can't we just use ethos?"

Alucard shook his head. "Zhey're 'ard to detect, vemember?"

He sighed and nodded. "Yeah. But what if it attacks you and I'm not there to help you?"

"Ve vill be close enough to speak telepavhically, no? If eizer of us needs 'elp, ve can veach out to vone anozzer."

Another sigh left him. Alucard *was* right about splitting up and covering more ground, and he *did* want to get this over with as quickly as possible, but after everything that happened—the dragon, the spiders, even everything in Atheson—he didn't want to leave Alucard's side. "I know, but I just…I can't stop worrying about you," he said sadly, pulling him closer.

Alucard smiled at him, placing his hand on the side of his neck. "I vorry about you, too, Zaliv, especially avter vhat 'appened vith zhose spiders. Ve can stay togezzer if you vant," he said softly, fiddling with his hair. "I just vhought you'd vant zhis over vith bevore dusk," he said with a small laugh.

Zalith smiled a little, too; he slid his hands to either side of his fiancé's waist and pulled him even closer. That was enough to arouse him. His heart beat faster, and his body tensed. He wanted him—of course he did. *Always*. But now really was not the time…even if he wasn't convinced that Alucard was avoiding having sex with him for whatever reason.

He couldn't be thinking about that right now, though. They had an egg to find and a fiend to avoid.

The demon dragged his hand over his face, sighed, and glanced around. "All right. But I want to be talking the whole time—not enough to distract each other, just…to make sure we know we're both okay."

Alucard nodded. "Okay. Ve can meet at zhe ozzer end of zhe lake."

He sighed again, his reluctance quickly constricting him. But he fought the urge to change his mind. "Just…please be careful."

"I vill. *You* be carevul, too."

Zalith nodded, but he didn't let go of Alucard.

The vampire scoffed amusedly. "You 'ave to let go vor me to go anyvhere."

He had to fight even harder. "Sorry," he said, faking a smile, and then he let go…but he quickly grabbed Alucard's waist again, pulling his body against his own, mostly out of worry, but there were hints of possessiveness, too—he couldn't help any of it. He kissed his lips and pressed his forehead against his. "I love you," he murmured, staring into the vampire's ice-blue eyes.

"I love you, too," Alucard said, caressing the side of the demon's face. "I'll be okay," he then tried to assure him. "Zhe moment I see anyving at all, I vill vetreat, okay?"

Zalith stared at him for a moment, his protective instincts devouring him, but he knew he couldn't cling to him right now, not if he wanted to bring this stupid quest to an end. So he nodded and said, "Okay. Let's get this over with."

Alucard nodded.

Still reluctant, still anxious…Zalith let go of his fiancé. "I'll see you soon," he said, the words like ice in his throat.

"Veally soon," Alucard said with a smile.

Zalith smiled as best he could. As he watched Alucard walk off, though, his heart raced harder. His worry grew heavier, so heavy that he stood there rooted in place, as frozen as the stretch of water in front of him. But he couldn't let it keep him there. He wouldn't be a prisoner of his emotions.

He huffed, rolling the tension from his shoulders before turning left along the lake's edge. The snow crunching beneath his boots was the only sound in a world hushed by cold. Frostbitten trees loomed along the bank, their skeletal limbs encased in ice, stretching like brittle claws towards the lake. Among them, frost-flowers clung to the frozen ground, delicate blue blossoms that shimmered with a faint glow.

For a heartbeat, they looked almost beautiful, tiny stars scattered across the white. But the longer Zalith's eyes lingered, the more their gleam seemed to pulse, as though in rhythm with some hidden breath beneath the ice. They felt less like plants and more like watchful things, quietly feeding on the silence around them.

He tore his gaze away and fixed it on the path ahead, keeping his senses sharp. The last thing he wanted was another surprise. He just needed to find this fiend egg, deliver it with the spider queen's blood, and then they could go home.

"*Alucard?*" he asked, speaking into his fiancé's mind.

"*I'm okay,*" the vampire replied. "*Noving yet. Vhat about you?*"

"*Nothing,*" he replied, looking around warily. "*What are these blue flowers?*"

"*Vrost blooms. Zhey are all part of vone big plant; zhe vlowers are like…eyes,*" he replied. "*Zhe body is usually under vater—zhis lake.*"

"*It doesn't eat people, does it?*"

"*No.*" He sounded amused. "*Small vings like vrogs and 'ares.*"

Zalith grimaced. "*Like a fly trap?*"

"*Sort of.*"

"*Ew.*"

"*Just try not to step on zhem. Zhey ooze zhis sort of silvery goo, vhich is like acid. Vill burn vhrough your boots.*"

"*Noted,*" Zalith replied, stepping over a cluster of the flowers.

And then quiet.

The demon scowled as the falling snow started to thicken. He focused on Alucard through their imprints, assessing his emotions—he was okay; no anxiety or fear or….

An idea crossed his mind. It was wrong and awful of him, but…Alucard's emotions weren't the only thing he could analyze right now. He could reach in deeper, he could read his thoughts, he could try to find out why he was hesitant about having sex.

Should he?

No.

Well….

No.

No?

He scowled at himself.

No.

He'd let Alucard tell him when he was ready.

And…not only was it terrible of him, but he was also still terrified of what the truth might be.

He dismissed the whole thing entirely.

There was nothing but white stretching ahead of him, an endless expanse of snow that swallowed everything in silence. The only signs of life he could sense were the sluggish fish trapped beneath the frozen skin of the lake, a twisting mass that must be the body of the giant plant Alucard mentioned, and his fiancé's steady aura on the far bank. No birds, no animals, no shifting in the trees…just stillness.

That was why the mound caught his eye—a misshapen rise breaking the flat monotony, a ripple in the snowfield where there should have been none. He narrowed his eyes as he trudged closer, every step more cautious than the last, and when he reached it, he circled the mound, studying it. From one angle, it looked ordinary, just a drift of snow pressed by the wind, but on the lake-facing side, a thick, half-buried branch was jutting out like a splintered bone.

Zalith crouched, brushed frost from it, and gripped it in one hand. His other instinctively drifted to the colt at his belt.

The moment he gave the branch a tug, the mound shuddered, snow shifting with a muffled crackle. His jaw tightened, shoulders tense. With a sharp yank, he pulled the branch free—and the entire heap collapsed in on itself, sending a spill of ice and snow hissing down the side.

He wasn't sure what he'd been expecting, really. There was nothing here.

With a sigh, he tucked the colt back into his belt, and as he continued his journey along the lake's bank, he spoke into Alucard's mind, *"Alucard?"*

His fiancé immediately replied, *"You zidn't see zhat, did you?"*

Zalith tensed up. *"See what?"*

"Noving."

"See what, Alucard? Are you okay?"

A pause.

"I slipped," the vampire admitted, clearly pouting.

Zalith exhaled in relief and let himself smile a little. *"Are you all right?"*

"Yes."

He loved Alucard's stubbornness. *"Do you need me to come over there and carry you, baby?"* he teased him.

"No," he grumbled.

"What did you slip on?"

"A stupid vock zhat 'ad no business being zhere."

Zalith couldn't help yet another chuckle. *"I'm sure it wasn't there just to spite you."*

"You zon't know zhat."

"Rocks aren't sentient."

"Some are."

The demon frowned. *"Really?"*

"You 'ave never seen a petramorph?"

"A what?"

"Petramorph. Is a sort of…armadillo…deer-looking mammal zhat 'as stone-looking armour. Zhey can voll up and disguise zhemselves as vocks."

His frown thickened. "*You're just messing with—*"

"*No, veally,*" Alucard interjected. "*You know 'ow sometimes you veel like you're being vatched? Could be a petramorph.*"

Zalith grimaced again. "*I'm not sure what's worse: stone-deer-armadillos or giant spiders…or goo-oozing flower eyeballs.*"

"*Velcome to Avalmoor, my love,*" the vampire replied, and he was clearly laughing.

The demon huffed, but he was smiling. He loved how much his fiancé knew about the world and its wildlife, and he loved their banter, too. He just wished he were with him right now. "*I literally cannot wait to leave this place,*" he replied as a sharp breeze raced past. He couldn't feel how cold it was—not the mundane cold—but as it ruffled his hair, he scowled irritably and fixed it with his hands.

Was there even a fiend here? Was this a waste of time? No. Alucard knew what he was doing. There *had* to be a fiend here…maybe he just wasn't looking hard enough.

A pair of birds cut across the sky, their wings stark against the pall of clouds. His gaze followed their path for a moment before he focused ahead again, exhaling through his nose, the breath steaming as he sighed.

Something caught his eye.

Not far away, crouched beneath the looming shadow of the mountains, stood a massive dead tree. Its branches clawed upward, and at its base yawned a dark hollow. As Zalith drew closer, the air soured; the pungent reek of rotting fish seeped from within, thick enough to sting his nose. That stench could only mean one thing.

He quickened his pace, dropping into a crouch as he reached the trunk. Peering into the gloom, his chest eased with relief. There it was: nestled in a crude bed of stones and decaying leaves lay a sky-blue egg, its surface faintly glimmering against the gloom, surrounded by half-eaten fish. That had to be it.

Still, Zalith wasn't one to take anything at face value. He spoke into Alucard's mind, "*I think I've found what we're looking for. I need you to come and see if it's actually a fiend egg.*"

"*I vill be vight over,*" Alucard replied.

The demon stood up and backed away from the tree; the pungent smell of fish was beginning to burn his eyes. He hadn't forgotten what Alucard had said, though. If this *was* the nest, the fiend was probably already on its way to kill him.

He scoured the area around him as best he could. The snow was falling harder, not far off a blizzard—

"Zhis is zhe egg."

Startled, Zalith sharply turned his head and looked down at Alucard, who was reaching into the nest. "Be careful," he insisted, moving closer.

But then the silence was shattered.

Heavy, thunderous footsteps pounded through the blizzard.

Zalith spun, his heart hammering against his ribs as he scoured the wall of white.

Then it burst into view—a hulking beast, seven feet of matted white fur and burning yellow eyes, barreling straight for them. His pulse spiked. In one fluid motion, he pulled the colt from his belt, gold flashing in his grip. He didn't wait, he didn't breathe; he levelled the barrel at the monster's chest and squeezed the trigger.

The fiend let out a horrified screech as the shot ripped through its arm—flesh, bone, and snow erupting in a wet explosion, and the severed limb thudded into the ice while the beast stumbled and skidded across the ground in a spray of frost.

Then silence.

It lay sprawled only feet away, motionless, its yellow eyes glazed and empty. Zalith kept the gun on it, refusing to lower his guard until he was certain.

Only when the stink of burnt powder and blood mixed in the cold air did his grip ease, and he lowered the weapon.

Relief flickered through him. Unlike the spiders, the fiend wouldn't be getting back up.

Alucard appeared at his side.

"Did you get the egg?" Zalith asked him.

The vampire nodded. "I sent to zhe vault. Zhat's a juvenal," he said, nodding down at the beast he'd just slain. "And a male."

Zalith smirked. "A what?"

"Juvenal…" Alucard repeated.

Amused, he laughed a little and said, "I think you mean juvenile."

The vampire pouted. "Vhatever. If 'e vas levt 'ere alone, zhe vemale must 'ave gone out 'unting."

"We should leave before she gets—"

Before he could finish speaking, the air split with a monstrous roar that shook the ground.

The mother.

Zalith had no interest in dealing with her. His gaze snapped to Alucard as he tucked the colt back into his belt, and then he seized the vampire's hand. "We're leaving."

Alucard didn't argue. In an instant, the vampire dematerialized them both into a rush of vermillion smoke. They surged skyward, abandoning the howling tundra below. Behind them, the grieving roar of the fiend's mother thundered through the storm, mourning her dead and stolen offspring as their figures vanished into the bleak, snow-choked sky.

| Alucard |

| Avalmoor, Drakalyth Region, Crytharion City |

Alucard landed outside Opus' house, rematerializing with Zalith at his side. He had no intention of spending any more time here than he had to. So he led the way up onto the porch and knocked on the door.

"Let's get this over with," the demon muttered with a sigh.

The door opened, and once again, the butler answered—this time, though, he was dressed in a maid's outfit and high heels. "Ah…Gerald White," he said, his voice as dead as ever. "This way," he said, turning around.

As they followed him into the house and down the hallway, the front door slammed shut on its own.

Alucard tried to relax, hoping he'd not have to see Opus' revolting brother again. That was the last thing he needed. But there was no sign or sound of him. Yet.

Once the butler-maid took them into Opus' office, Alucard sighed and slumped down onto the couch. He hadn't failed to notice Zalith's scowl, though, and despite knowing the answer, he asked anyway, "Are you okay?"

"I'm okay," the demon replied, sitting beside him. "I just don't want to talk to Opus."

Alucard shrugged and rested his head on his mate's shoulder. "Vell, at least ve only 'ave to see 'im zhis vinal time, and zhen never again vor vhat I 'ope is a very long time."

Zalith sighed again. "The bracelet I got for the dragon is only going to fit her for so long, unfortunately."

"Vell…ve could just get zhat vesized. Any jeweller could take and turn into someving else, too. Ve zon't 'ave to buy 'er someving new and get enchanted."

"Will that ruin the enchantment?"

"No. You could take each individual link on zhat bracelet and use zhem all on divverent vings, and zhey vould all veceive zhe enchantment. Zhe only vay to vemove an enchantment is vith zhe same ethos used to cast," he explained.

"How do you know that?" the demon asked, smirking.

"Zhat's vhat Soren does—'e enchants zhe metal and zhen makes into jewellery. I assume vould vork zhat vay. If 'e could do zhese enchantments vor anyving but zemons, ve vouldn't 'ave even 'ad to come to Opus," he grumbled.

Their conversation ended when the door to the left of the desk opened.

Opus stepped into the room. "Either fiend eggs have diminished to the size of trinkets fit for a waistcoat pocket, or you bring me tidings I would much prefer not to hear, yes," the angel drawled, reclining against the edge of his desk as his gaze settled upon them.

Alucard snarled irritably. "Ve got vhat you asked vor."

"Have you done what *we* asked for?" Zalith questioned.

Opus extended his hand with a languid flick of the wrist. "The recompense, if you please—let us not tarry in ceremony, yes."

Alucard got up and reached into his pocket; from his vault, he took the green-filled syringe he'd used to extract blood from the spider leg earlier. Then, he handed it to Opus.

Opus accepted it with a faint nod. "Most obliging. And the egg, yes?"

The vampire extended his hand to the side, twisting his palm downward. His gaze never left the angel, a flat, vacant stare locking him in place. A second later, the enormous sky-blue egg materialized and slammed onto the floor beside him with a wet, resounding squelch. Slime burst from its surface in all directions, spattering across the polished floor and streaking up the legs of Opus' desk. The shell itself held intact, gleaming obscenely through its sheen of viscous muck, Alucard's silent way of ensuring the offering was as inconvenient as it was undeniable.

Opus grimaced, looking as if he might gag…but he forced a smile as his gaze fell upon it. "Exquisite…yes…. Quite…beyond expectation."

"Zhe jewellery," Alucard requested.

The angel's smile lingered, tight and genteel, as he placed the blood-filled syringe on his desk. "But of course. Efficiency is a virtue, and you two seem to possess it in spades. Far swifter than the rabble I am accustomed to dealing with—almost a shame I cannot retain you permanently, yes—"

"We're only here to trade with you, sorry," Zalith said with that condescending smile.

Reaching into one of his desk's drawers, Opus let out a short, derisive breath. "Well, should you ever reconsider—"

"We won't," Zalith cut in.

The angel's lips thinned, but he said nothing further. Instead, he turned and laid a delicate array upon the desk before them: the thin chain, Alucard's new ring, the collars, and the baby bracelet. "Your effects…enchanted as stipulated, yes. Wrought with the utmost care."

"Thank you," the demon said, taking all of them, and as he handed Alucard his ring, he looked back at the angel. "A pleasure doing business with you."

"Now, about the Lumendatt," Opus said smoothly, folding his hands behind his back. "When, pray, ought I to expect its arrival, yes?"

"Vhen ve decide," Alucard snarled as he put his new ring onto his right index finger. "Now, vhether you mind or not," he mocked with Opus' forced tone, "ve 'ave places to be."

The vampire took Zalith's hand and left Opus' office before the angel had a chance to respond. They headed through the house and to the front door, which Alucard yanked open with an irritated hiss. Then, when they were finally on the street again, he huffed sharply and tried to relax.

"Are you okay?" Zalith asked quietly, smiling a little.

Alucard huffed again. "Is very 'ard to vesist zhe urge to kill 'im."

"I know," the demon said, squeezing his hand.

Once they were a comfortable distance from the house, the vampire sighed and stopped walking. "Do you vant to do anyving…or should ve just go straight 'ome? 'As been a long day."

"It has," Zalith agreed. "At least we got what we came for, though," he added, smiling again. "Let's head home."

Nodding, Alucard moved his arms around him, and then he dematerialized. They'd not have to come back here for a long, long time if ever, and that thought alone was a *great* comfort.

Chapter Eighteen

— ⸱ ✝ ⸱ —

Home At Last

| Alucard |
| *Aestrael, Uzlia Isles, Usrul, Castle Reiner* |

By the time they crossed the castle threshold, Alucard had barely set a hand to the clasp of his coat when the noise reached them: a sharp, ragged scuffle carried down the hall—metal clashing, feet skidding, squeaking half-snarls—and through it all, what was unmistakably Edwin's voice rang out, strained with effort.

What was going on?

As Zalith hastily led the way through the entrance hall, Alucard followed him. They hurried through the lounge, the library, and the *main* hall. A sharp turn into the ballroom brought the source of the commotion into view.

Edwin was pinned against the wall beside the stage, a dented stew pot jammed over his head like a makeshift helm. In one trembling hand, he clutched a saucepan, and in the other was a spatula, both rattling with his shivers. At his feet, the dragonlet squeaked and chirped, wings flaring as if she were the most fearsome beast alive, snapping at him with all the menace her tiny body could muster.

"Thank the heavens you're here, sirs!" the butler called with a brief glance at them. "She's trying to eat me!" he panicked, standing on one leg, pointing down at the baby dragon with his spatula.

Clearly amused, Zalith smiled and laughed as he made his way over. "Don't worry about that. She doesn't have teeth yet," he said, scooping her up in his arms, and she chirped happily and nuzzled his face in response.

Edwin sighed in relief. "Thank you," he breathed, wiping the sweat from his forehead with his sleeve. "One more second and she would have chewed through my boots!" he insisted.

"I doubt it," the demon said with a smile, petting the dragonlet's head. "But thank you, Edwin. I'll adjust your pay accordingly to accommodate the stress you've been through."

Calming down, the butler sighed. "Thank you, sirs," he said, bowing humbly.

"When did she last eat?" Zalith asked.

"About twenty minutes ago, sir, which is what I think prompted her attack. She may still be hungry."

The demon nodded. "Prepare her some more food and I'll feed her upstairs in my office."

"Of course, sir," he said, and then he left the ballroom.

Zalith turned to face Alucard.

"She veally 'as a personality," the vampire said, and when she noticed that he was looking down at her, the dragonlet hissed at him.

The demon smiled. "She does, doesn't she?" he agreed. "We need to work on her manners, though. I don't believe there are dragon training classes around here, are there?" he asked, smirking.

Alucard shook his head. "Vell, since she sees you as 'er parent, maybe vill be a lot simpler to train 'er. Dragonlets are very obedient to zheir parents, even Aegis."

Zalith shrugged as he began leading the way back into the main hall. "I hope so. Right now, I'm just focused on getting her adjusted and on a schedule—I need to do more research."

The vampire stopped when they reached the library. "Vell… zhere are probably some books in 'ere zhat could help," he suggested, looking around at the shelves upon shelves of books.

"I'll get around to it sometime tonight."

They navigated the castle halls, eventually reaching the tower that led up to Zalith's office. Alucard pushed the door open; he went over to the couch, and as he slumped down, he watched Zalith go to his desk.

The demon set the dragonlet on the floor, but she instantly began chirping in protest and scurried straight back to him. Hopping at his legs, she clawed for attention, and as Zalith took the new jewellery from his pockets to place on the table, she hooked her tiny wing-talons into the fabric of his trousers and began climbing, scaling him with determined little scrabbles until she reached his waist.

Alucard watched with quiet adoration as Zalith sighed, gently peeling the dragonlet off his waist and setting her in the chair behind him. For a moment, it seemed settled—until she pounced again, talons latching onto either side of his ass. The demon froze in flat disbelief while Alucard smirked, amused all the more because he could see the truth in Zalith's eyes: beneath the deadpan mask, he was entertained.

With a stubborn determination, the dragonlet scrabbled her way up his back, and Zalith only exhaled another weary sigh, waiting for her to crest his shoulder. When she finally did, he plucked her free and let her cling to his chest instead, draped across him like some absurd, living necklace.

Alucard smiled, lounging on the couch. "She veally loves you, Zaliv."

The demon exhaled deeply as he slowly sank into his seat. "I think you're right." He looked down at her and frowned. "I'm not very nice, you know."

She chirped in response and nuzzled her face into his neck.

"Maybe she likes zhat you're mean…maybe makes 'er veel safe," Alucard suggested.

Zalith laughed as he picked up the baby bracelet and unclipped it. "Maybe. She wouldn't be the first one," he said as he put the bracelet around the dragon's neck.

Alucard frowned. "Vhat does zhat mean?"

"People feel safe around me because they know I'm mean enough to get the job done," he explained, smiling across the room at the vampire once he'd secured the bracelet. "Look at Greymore, for example. He could have run long ago, but he was smart and knew who to rely on, even though there have admittedly been more than a few bumps in the road along the way."

"Everyvone velies on you. You're veally good at vhat you do vor people. None of us vould be safe 'ere if veren't vor you, you know."

"Actually, no one would be safe here if it weren't for *you*," the demon replied matter-of-factly. "You're the one who put all the protection around the castle and the islands, and frankly, if you weren't here, I probably would have died in Eltaria."

Alucard shrugged a little, gazing at him. "Ve're both safe because of each ozzer."

Zalith nodded. "So, I guess it was meant to be, then."

The vampire smiled. "Yes."

Once the dragonlet finally lost interest and busied herself with her bracelet, Zalith rose from his chair and crossed the room.

Alucard's smirk deepened as the demon came closer. He caught hold of Zalith's collar and tugged him down until their faces nearly touched. For a heartbeat, he simply gazed at him—those dark, infuriatingly perfect features—before closing the space with a kiss. He'd been aching for this small closeness since they returned home, and when Zalith answered with his own kiss, the ache eased into something far hungrier. As their mouths lingered together, Zalith slid down onto the couch, pressing his body against Alucard's. The warmth and weight of him stoked Alucard's anticipation, tightening in his chest and clawing deeper the longer he let himself stay in it.

A faint frown tugged at Alucard's lips even as he kissed him, a flicker of frustration at how quickly the slow burn was unravelling into arousal. His heat left every nerve raw, every desire sharpened, and he couldn't hold himself back. He hooked his leg over

Zalith's, dragging him closer until their bodies pressed flush. Zalith smirked against his mouth, as if amused by how easily the vampire's restraint was slipping, and let his hand trail down the length of Alucard's body. When his fingers reached his waist, he tugged his shirt free, slipping his hand beneath the fabric to claim bare skin, his palm gliding possessively across him as though he had every right to it.

A rush of exhilaration surged through Alucard, quickening his heartbeat until it pounded in his chest. Their kisses turned hungrier, edged with urgency, and he felt the thrill coil hot in his veins. Zalith's hand slid higher, lingering over his abs before claiming his chest, fingers pressing with a teasing squeeze as a smirk ghosted across his lips. Alucard felt Zalith's hardening dick pressed against his thigh, and the contact sent a spark racing through him, stoking his own desire into something fierce, something he finally felt he could give in to.

But when Zalith's hand slipped lower, brushing past his waist, the disheartening weight of hesitation seized him. Embarrassment crawled up his spine, the what-ifs clawing at his mind—what if he disappointed again, what if he failed again? The shame hollowed him out, dimming the heat that had been building until his body felt like stone, eager yet unyielding. The hunger of moments before faded to a still, quiet gloom.

Then—sudden and sharp—pain lanced through his side. Alucard winced, snarling under his breath as he flinched and snapped his gaze downward. There, with her wing-arms braced against the cushion, Zalith's dragonlet bared her toothless mouth, having nipped at his waist.

Zalith gently pushed her back down to the floor. "No," he said sternly.

After she chirped quietly and shot a glare at Alucard, she wandered off, returning to Zalith's desk.

"Are you okay?" the demon asked, looking down at Alucard.

Pouting, Alucard scowled. "Vhy does she keep doing zhat?" he grumbled.

"Maybe it's because of the gold," he said, fiddling with Alucard's hair.

"You vear gold and she zoesn't bite you."

"Because *I'm* her Mommy," the demon said, smiling. "If it's not the gold, then maybe it's just who she is—Edwin was terrified of her."

Alucard sighed and shrugged. "Is just…most animals alvays love me," he mumbled, glancing over at her—

As they locked eyes, she immediately hissed.

The vampire looked back up at Zalith. "She 'ates me and vill probably try to eat me vhile I sleep."

Zalith laughed. "Maybe…but I won't let her. I'm sure she'll come around in time; you two just need to spend more time together. She's only been alive for two days, remember."

"I know," he muttered.

"Things will be fine," Zalith assured him. Then, he looked at the dragonlet. "Come here," he said, patting the side of the couch.

Without hesitation, she hurried along the floor, and once she reached him, Zalith sat, picked her up, and held her in his arms.

"Say sorry," he told her, holding her out to Alucard, who also sat up.

Alucard stared down at her, and for a moment, she glared at him, sniffing—but then she hissed again.

"See, she's sorry," Zalith said with a smile, cradling her.

The vampire sighed and slumped back. "Vight."

A quiet knock then came at the door.

"Yes?" Zalith called.

Edwin stepped in, carrying a food-filled syringe in his right hand. "For the baby, sir," he said, making his way over, keeping a cautious eye on the dragonlet.

"Thank you," the demon said, taking it from him.

The butler swiftly left the room, pulling the door shut behind him.

Zalith got up and went to his desk, where he sat and started feeding the dragonlet.

Alucard pouted. Clearly, their moment together was over. "I'm going to go and make a start on zhat dragon vur," he grumbled, standing up.

"Why are you grumpy?" the demon asked.

He shrugged as he headed to the door. "I'm not. You're busy, so I vill go and do someving until you're done. She clearly zoesn't vant me in 'ere."

"Of course, you can do what you want, but *I* want you here," the demon said softly.

Alucard stopped by the door and looked back at him. He didn't *want* to leave, but he *did* want to work on the dragon fur, and he couldn't exactly bring it up into Zalith's office. So, he frowned in confliction and said, "You zon't vant me to bring zhat up 'ere. I'm sure you zon't vant vur all over your ovvice. But vhen you're done vith 'er, you could come and join me in my study?"

"Okay," Zalith said with a content smile. "As long as dragon stuff doesn't get on me."

Amused, Alucard smirked. "I vill protect you vrom all zhe dragon stuff."

"Thank you. Do you think being near the fur will traumatize the baby?" he then asked, looking down at the dragonlet latched onto his chest.

"Maybe," the vampire mumbled. "I zon't vant 'er to 'ate me any more zhan she alveady does…. Maybe you can try to put 'er to sleep bevore you come down."

"She usually falls asleep after she eats, so it shouldn't take too long."

Alucard nodded. "Okay. I vill see you zhen."

Zalith smiled and focused on feeding the dragonlet.

And Alucard left his office. He had a lot of work ahead of him, and he was eager to make a start.

Chapter Nineteen

— ⸲ † ⸱ —

Disconsolate

| Alucard |
| *Uzlia Isles, Usrul, Castle Reiner* |

In his study, Alucard sat cross-legged on the floor, the white dragon pelt spread before him like a pale shroud. He'd already burned away the remnants of blood, bone, and flesh with controlled fire, leaving only the soft, silken fur behind. Now, he carefully trimmed away neat portions, each cut and tuft set aside for the many things he intended to craft.

He wasn't sure how long he'd been working before Zalith came into the room with a small straw basket in his arms. He stopped cutting the fur and glanced at him, watching as he carefully placed the basket down on the nearby couch, and considering how gentle his mate was being, he assumed that the dragonlet must be inside.

"How's it going?" Zalith asked, making his way over to him.

Alucard focused on the fur and the knife in his hand. "Is going okay. I'm just cutting into smaller pieces vor later."

Zalith frowned, looking revolted—

"Is clean," Alucard assured him. "I purged of all germs and nastiness," he mocked with an amused smile.

"Thank you," his mate said.

The vampire glanced up at him. He could see Zalith trying to hide his smile.

"How long do you think this will take?" the demon asked curiously.

Shrugging, Alucard cut off another square of fur and placed it on the pile beside him. "A vew more hours, maybe…but I vill probably stop soon and vesume tomorrow. Is getting late." He was tired, and his head was starting to ache…again.

Zalith sat down beside him. "What are you going to do with the leftovers?"

"I 'ave a lot planned. I zon't know if zhere vill be any levt."

"What are you planning to do with it all?"

He smirked and said, "Zhat's a secret."

"A secret for me?" Zalith asked, smiling.

"Maybe," he said with a shrug, cutting off another square of fur.

Zalith laughed quietly. "I'm looking forward to it."

Alucard put the piece aside, and then he placed down his knife. "Do you vant to vind Peaches and Sabazios vith me and put zheir new collars on?" he asked, turning his gaze to Zalith.

"Okay," the demon agreed.

As they stood up, Alucard glanced at the basket on the couch. "Are you taking 'er vith you?"

He headed to the couch. "Yeah. I don't want to leave her by herself."

"'Opevully she zoesn't vake up and 'iss at Sabazios again," he said, looking down at the sleeping dragonlet as Zalith carefully picked the basket up.

"I'm sure she will. Hissing seems to be one of her favourite things to do," the demon said, smirking as he led the way out of Alucard's study. "I just hope everyone learns to get along."

"Vell, I'm sure Peaches and Sabazios vill take to 'er. As vor my chickens… and my snake… I zon't know. She might vink zhey're dinner."

"That's fine," Zalith said as they headed for one of the garden doors. "I don't imagine she'll be near the coop or in the terrarium any time soon, anyway."

Alucard nodded.

In the garden, Sabazios was chasing a squirrel. The moment the hellhound took his eyes off it to look their way, though, the creature darted up a tree. After a disappointed huff, the hound raced over to them, skidding to a halt in front of them moments later.

Zalith lifted the basket slightly to keep him from investigating its contents.

Alucard smiled and scratched the hellhound's ears. "Vhat 'ave you been up to out 'ere?" he asked as the hound panted happily.

Zalith handed him Sabazios' new collar.

Once Alucard put it around the hound's neck, he patted his head and smiled. Sabazios barked happily but then turned his attention to Zalith, staring at him with an expectant look on his face. The demon smiled and petted the dog's head, and as he did, Sabazios sat down and panted contently.

"Suits 'im," Alucard said, making sure the collar was secure.

"Yeah, it looks good. You picked the right one," Zalith agreed.

"'Ave you seen Peaches?" the vampire then asked Sabazios.

The hound barked and stared up at him. He *hadn't* seen Peaches.

Alucard said to Zalith, "Ve should go and look vor 'er."

"Okay. Have *you* seen her today?"

"No," he said as they turned around and headed back towards the doors. "She's probably in zhe sunvoom, zhough."

They walked through the castle to the sunroom, and when they stepped inside, Peaches, who was sleeping on one of the couches, raised her head and gawped at them, flicking her tail around while she watched as they approached.

Zalith smiled and said, "She's probably been in here all day."

"She veally likes sitting in zhe sun," Alucard said as the demon handed him Peaches' new collar. "Vank you."

Peaches stood up and stretched. Alucard crouched in front of her, pulled off her current collar, and put the new chain on her. She purred loudly, rubbing her face eagerly against his stubbly chin, and once he was done, he gently eased her away and scratched her ears. She sat down and prodded the diamond chain with her paw for a few moments before curling up again.

"Vell, she seems to like," the vampire said.

"She looks good," Zalith agreed.

Alucard then turned to face his mate. "Vhat do you vant to do now?"

Zalith sighed. "I don't know."

"Vell...ve could go and sit in zhe lounge until dinner is veady," he suggested.

Zalith nodded. "Sounds good."

All the back and forth was starting to make Alucard feel...odd. They were in Zalith's office...and then the garden—no...before they went outside, they were in Alucard's study. Then the sunroom, now the lounge.

Alucard sighed tiredly, closing his eyes as he tried to relax on the couch.

Zalith carefully placed the basket at the other end of the couch, and then he made himself comfortable beside Alucard.

However, the demon couldn't seem to settle for very long. Alucard watched as he lifted his head and looked over at the basket. The dragonlet was still sleeping, wrapped up in a fluffy black blanket.

The demon relaxed against him, resting his forehead on Alucard's as a slow smile spread across his face. "Shall we continue where we left off earlier?"

Alucard's lips curved, the answer slipping out before thought could catch it, "Okay." Already his body was taut with desire, the restless fire of his heat coiling tight inside him, sending jolts of anticipation racing through every nerve.

Zalith's grin widened before he closed the distance, kissing him with a hunger that made Alucard's heart race. He slid a hand to the back of Zalith's head, tangling in his hair, tugging him closer. Their mouths moved together, slow at first but charged, each brush of lips sparking hotter longing. Zalith's hand wasted no time, slipping beneath his shirt, his warm palm dragging across Alucard's skin in a way that made him stifle quiet hums. He arched closer, eager for the contact, his excitement rising with every press of the demon's body. His leg hooked over Zalith's, pulling him flush, chest to chest as the kiss deepened, threatening to unravel him entirely.

The demon laughed against his lips, his hand roaming up over Alucard's abs until it found his chest. His fingers grazed the vampire's left pec, and then he pinched his nipple. Alucard jolted with a sharp flinch, a pout pulling at his lips as he scowled in protest, only to hear Zalith's amused chuckle. The vampire barely had time to linger in his fluster before Zalith claimed his mouth again, his kiss quick and insistent. His hand slipped free from beneath Alucard's shirt to toy with the buttons; one by one, they came undone beneath his deft fingers, and with each inch of exposure, Alucard's pulse hammered harder. The heat inside him burned into eagerness; all that mattered was feeling him— skin, warmth, and affection… his desperation for it was blinding.

Alucard exhaled a long, shaky breath as Zalith's lips trailed from his mouth to his throat, then lower, brushing heat across his chest. A smile tugged faintly at the vampire's lips; he combed his fingers through Zalith's hair, soaking in the closeness. For a heartbeat, he wanted more—he *craved* it. But then Zalith's hand slipped down, his fingertips stroking his waist, and all at once, the spark soured. The eager warmth twisted into a hollow ache, his mind clouding with the old, gnawing voice that told him he wasn't enough. Not the right body. Not a real man like Zalith deserved.

His heart sank. The moment that had felt so intoxicating seconds ago now pressed against him like a weight. He frowned, conflicted, shifting restlessly before gently catching Zalith's wrist, halting him before the buckle of his belt.

And just like that, the moment broke.

Zalith's sigh was soft but edged with disappointment, his expression dimming as he sat up. "Sorry," he muttered, the word clipped—and Alucard could swear there was a trace of annoyance buried in his tone.

Alucard pushed himself upright, his shoulders tight and his gaze fixed on his lap. Anxiety knotted in his chest, a messy tangle of guilt, worry, and shame. He knew he was letting Zalith down—maybe even angering him—and the thought only made it worse. No matter how many times he tried, no matter how many times Zalith tried, he always froze once things went further than kissing and touch. The words to explain it wouldn't come; the apology stuck in his throat. Instead, silence pressed down on him like a shroud.

He let his head hang, shame settling heavy in his gut. Frustration burned beneath it. His instincts screamed for Zalith, his body ached with craving, but every time he tried to follow through, something inside him locked up. It felt like being trapped between hunger and refusal, and the longer it went on, the more unbearable the dissonance became.

Why couldn't he just... *tell him*? He wanted to. He *needed* to. Zalith deserved to know why he kept doing this. But the embarrassment...the *fear*...and the lack of answers. It all kept him in a suffocating, tight hold.

Zalith slouched back, silently staring across the room at the arched windows, watching as the dull, grey sky darkened outside.

Alucard didn't like the silence *at all*. He had to say something. So he looked at his mate...but when he noticed his despondent stare, he felt his heart break. He was upsetting him, *hurting* him, and he hated himself for it.

He looked back down at his lap. "I'm sorry," he murmured. "I just...zon't veally veel like vight now." Maybe if he took some time to just sit somewhere and find the words...and the courage...then maybe he could tell Zalith what he was struggling with.

The demon sighed in what sounded like defeat. "That's okay," he uttered.

Alucard glanced at him again, trying to work out what to say. "Did you...vink of name vor zhe dragonlet yet?"

"No," the demon answered.

"Do you still vant me to vink of some more?"

"If you want to," Zalith said, his sullen tone thickening.

The vampire frowned guiltily. He could hear the sadness and disappointment in Zalith's voice. Why couldn't he just get over these anxious thoughts so that he could stop hurting the man he loved?

And then, a common occurrence as of late, a knock came at the door.

Alucard looked over to see Edwin standing in the doorway.

"Dinner is ready, sirs," the butler called.

Zalith shifted his gaze to him. "Okay. Thank you," he muttered.

Alucard followed the demon through the castle once more. They didn't utter a word to one another.

Once they reached their private dining room and sat at the table, the silence remained.

Alucard hated it, but he didn't know what to say.

'*I'm hesitant about having sex because I'm not a real man.*'

'*I can't stop thinking about the fact that I can't make you cum; what real man can't do that?*'

'*I feel disgusting and strange and odd. I'm worried that you'll feel the same way eventually.*'

'*Damien would absolutely love this, to see me lose you after everything we've been through because you realized I really am the revolting, pathetic little thing Damien says I am.*'

'*I don't know who or what I am, and that scares me. I don't know where to find the answers.*'

It wasn't that hard, was it?

He *thought* he was about to speak, but his heart started racing. Painfully so. Because the heavier thoughts hit him next. He wasn't a man, and Zalith wanted a man, not some…odd thing that wasn't one or the other. He'd surely decide that soon enough, wouldn't he?

Alucard tried to keep a dismayed scowl off his face. He stared down at his plate when it arrived, trying to calm his racing thoughts. But his attempts were futile. The fear and despair wouldn't let him speak.

Zalith didn't say anything either.

And in that same silence, they ate their food.

Alucard hoped that Zalith might say something, but the minutes ticked by, and his heart ached a little more each time he glanced at his mate.

Something then came to him. "Did you put your new chain on?"

"Not yet," the demon said flatly.

Alucard looked down at his plate again. "Do you veel better zhan earlier? Avter zhe spiders."

Zalith shrugged.

The vampire frowned. He wanted to ask him what was wrong, but he already knew the answer. Trying to start a conversation and move away from the sadness was useless, too. He couldn't solve this with deflection.

And he didn't want to eat anymore.

He put his knife and fork down and leaned back in his seat with his glass of wine. The movement aggravated his body, though; a strange, cold sensation spiralled through him, and his head started aching.

Zalith sighed quietly—

"I'm going to go upstairs," Alucard interjected. It was probably better that he was alone with these feelings…and with this struggle. "I just vant to lie down—I vill…vait in bed vor you," he said, placing his glass down. Maybe the solitude would help him prepare for the inevitable conversation. But he wasn't hopeful. He knew what he was like.

"Okay," the demon said as Alucard stood up. "I'll be up eventually."

Alucard didn't ask what that meant. He knew.

He left the dining room, ignoring the worsening ache in his head and made his way up to the bedroom. After collapsing onto the bed, he closed his eyes and tried to relax. But how could he relax while he was actively hurting Zalith? Confusing him, *starving* him. Things would only get worse if he didn't speak up—and *that* was what was so fucking frustrating about it. He *knew* that he needed to tell Zalith, and he *wanted* to…but he just…couldn't. He froze up, he hesitated, he let the fear and panic and anxiety get the better of him. He was so fucking stupid and annoying and pathetic.

Pathetic.

How much longer would it be until Zalith confronted him? Would he be able to tell him what was going on if his mate *demanded* answers?

What answers, though? Alucard still didn't have them all. He still didn't know why or what or where or when.

He scowled in despair and crawled under the covers. He didn't know what to do anymore. Would he get the answers? Would he remember the things he desperately needed to? The things that would help him clear this whole mess up.

All he could do was try.

Maybe… *this* time, he'd relive those moments; maybe he'd remember what he was, maybe he'd remember when he chose or if he chose at all.

And maybe… things would be better tomorrow.

THE NUMEN CHRONICLES
SERIES ONE

Nosferatu
The Numen Chronicles | Volume 1

Demon's Fate
The Numen Chronicles | Volume 2

Light
The Numen Chronicles | Volume 3

Demon's Bane
The Numen Chronicles | Volume 4

Forbidden Bond
The Numen Chronicles | Companion Story

Ascendant
The Numen Chronicles | Volume 5

The Silver Claw
The Numen Chronicles | Interlude Story

The Hunt for Niedreid
The Numen Chronicles | Interlude Story

The Keeper's Realm
The Numen Chronicles | Tether Story

Icarus
The Numen Chronicles | Volume 6

Demon's Curse
The Numen Chronicles | Volume 7

Renascence
The Numen Chronicles | Volume 8

Demon's Reclamation
The Numen Chronicles | Volume 9

[And more...]

THE NUMENVERSE
OTHER SERIES/STORIES

Aldergrove Chronicles

Set in the year 1176 after Aegisguard's second world war. After being told he has only six months left to live, Clementine decides to track down his sister's murderers, leading him to Aldergrove Academy, a place where a hundred students must fight to the death to earn their right to travel to the New World. But he soon learns that the students aren't the only ones prowling the corridors at night in search of blood.

Where The Wild Wolves Have Gone

Set in the year 1330. Following Luan, a young transman werewolf who belongs to a pack owned by Lyca Corp., a military-focused organization. The pack have served them for generations, but after a mission goes sideways, Luan begins to learn the horrifying truth about the people they serve.

Greykin Chronicles

Set in the year 1332, following Jackson, a journalist who heads to the snowy mountains of Ascela in search of his missing best friend, Wilson. But he discovers that not only is there a whole different world hidden out there, but death isn't necessarily the end for some creatures.

The Numen Chronicles Series Two

Set in the year 1335. While hunting for his missing friend, Elijah stumbles upon a fiery journalist, who so happens to be looking for the same people as him: the doctors who experimented on him when he was a child. But when the two are forced to go on the run together, Elijah's healing wounds are opened, and he realizes that Lyca Corp. took more than his childhood.

To stay up to date with future releases, follow the author through their website!

www.numenverse.com/

Discover more at www.numenverse.com